TERROR AT THE FAIR

TERROR AT THE FAIR

A Snap Malek Mystery

Robert Goldsborough

MYSTERIOUSPRESS.COM

INTEGRATED MEDIA
NEW YORK

Copyright © 2011 by Robert Goldsborough

ISBN: 978-1-5040-7836-8

This edition published in 2022 by MysteriousPress.com/Open Road Integrated Media, Inc.
180 Maiden Lane
New York, NY 10038
www.openroadmedia.com

To my Granddaughters Five:

Lillian Rose, Violet Marie, Charlotte Elizabeth,

Gretchen Jane, and Madeleine Elizabeth

The Chicago Railroad Fair, held in the summer and early fall of 1948 and 1949, commemorated the 100th anniversary of the city's first train service. Said to be the last great rail exposition held in the U.S., the fair was mounted on a narrow, 50-acre strip along Lake Michigan some two miles south of the city's Loop business district.

Although hastily arranged during the winter and spring of 1948, the fair quickly gained the support and participation of 38 railroads, many of them eager to use the event as a way of promoting and revitalizing passenger traffic and displaying new equipment in the aftermath of World War II.

The popularity of the fair in 1948 emboldened its organizers to bring it back for a second year, much as the city's Century of Progress World's Fair fifteen years earlier was held over for a second year based on the success of the first.

TERROR AT THE FAIR

PROLOGUE

He had laid the last of the iron bars in place across the rails, making sure that their positioning was such that the ancient and relatively lightweight locomotive would surely derail and crash, taking with it the open-side excursion coaches crowded with fair-goers. He checked his watch again: twenty minutes before the next train was due, and it always ran on schedule.

This was the darkest stretch along the line, so the lethal bars on the track wouldn't be seen by some chance passerby, not that people walked in this remote area of the fairgrounds anyway.

His work done, he stepped back into a cluster of bushes and knelt to wait, feeling the bulge in his hip pocket. It was comforting to have it there, although it seemed beyond the realm of possibility that it would be needed. No, this would be simple and efficient, the final act in his crusade.

It is almost over now, Papa. Just a few more minutes . . .

He heard something—footsteps? No, it was probably just leaves on a tree along the tracks rustling in the breezes that wafted in off Lake Michigan on the August night. There they were again, louder this time. Definitely footsteps! Perhaps one of the janitorial crew. They were very good about picking up rubbish. Whoever it was would have moved on long before the train came along.

He saw the beam of light before he saw the figure. A silhouetted man carrying a flashlight was slowly walking along the tracks, playing the light back and forth, back and forth, until its yellow halo rested upon the iron bars. The interloper with the flashlight squatted down to study the bars, then began picking them up and tossing them off the tracks.

He rose from his crouch in the bushes and wrapped his hand around the pistol in his jacket pocket. He walked toward the man, whom he now recognized, and called to him by name, pulling the weapon out. So now, one more must die.

CHAPTER ONE

June 1949

"Snap, don't you get tired of the grind around here? Same old thing every day and all?" Chief of Detectives Fergus Sean Fahey eyed me from under bushy, almost-white eyebrows, leaning back in his battered chair and taking a deep drag on a Lucky Strike from the pack I had dropped on his desk blotter, as had been my daily habit for years.

"Why Fergus, how can you say that? I look forward to these lively and stimulating conversations with you each morning. That alone is enough to make me want to drag myself out of bed and make the trip in from Oak Park on that creaky old Elevated every day. Besides, I haven't been around forever, even if it seems to be the case to you. All the others upstairs have logged more years here than I have."

The old cop grunted. "That may be true, but none of those

three has the slightest shred of ambition." He was referring to the trio of beat reporters on the other Chicago daily papers who, like me, had desks one flight up in the drab press room at Chicago Police Headquarters, 1121 S. State St. They were: Anson Masters of the *Daily News*; Dirk O'Farrell of the *Sun-Times*; and Packy Farmer of the *Herald-American*.

"Shoot, I'm guessing that you generate seventy-per cent of all the news that comes out of this weather-beaten old building," Fahey went on, taking a last puff on his Lucky and grinding out the butt in his tin ashtray. "All they do is grab onto your coat-tails. You get the news, then feed it to them like a mother robin giving worms to her brood in the nest. They each ought to be giving you a slice of their salaries."

"I'll admit I've got the best beat in the building, all right. Which is to say, your very own Detective Bureau, the heart and soul of the force, where most of the really good stuff is—murder, extortion, bribery, mob mischief—all of the things that our noble readers crave and devour. But in truth, it cuts both ways. I get stories from the other boys on their beats as well."

"Not very damned many, as far as I can tell," Fahey snorted, running a thick hand through thin hair. "But why in hell am I trying to tell you your business? If anyone has stayed at the party too long, it's got to be me."

"Now Fergus, I've been hearing your 'It's time for me to walk off into the sunset' routine for years now. We both know you love it here, for all the rhapsodizing I hear about that cottage of yours up in Wisconsin. After six months in those woods on that lake, you would be figuring out ways to un-retire. Don't try to deny it."

"I'm willing to give that life a try," he said defiantly, crossing beefy arms over his chest.

"You are? If that's the case, when are you turning in your

resignation? That would make one heck of a good story for our readers."

I had called his bluff, and he gave me a crooked smile. "Well . . . things are in turmoil in the department right now, so until everything gets straightened out . . ."

He let the sentence hang and I paused a beat, then another. I'd been here with him before. "Okay, how long do you think it will take to get things 'straightened out'?" I posed.

"No comment," he snarled. "Are you down here to bedevil me or to play newspaper reporter?"

"Point taken, Fergus. What's going on? As you can see, my pencil is poised."

"Oddly enough, things are very quiet today," he muttered, shuffling through papers at the top of the heap littering his desk. "Nothing here that would interest your fine *Chicago Tribune* readers, or the readers of those other rags represented by your colleagues upstairs." He made the word "colleagues" sound like a synonym for leprosy.

"So first you tempt me by suggesting you have something worth writing about, and when I ask what it is, you dash my hopes by telling me that your cupboard is empty, with not a single tidbit inside. I'm both disappointed and dismayed, Fergus. Well, thanks for your time. The boys upstairs are going to be disappointed as well."

"No doubt they will. But as I said before, it's still a good thing they've got you—and will have you for a long time to come." If only that had been true.

I went back up to the press room to find that everybody was back from their respective beats around the building. As I walked in, they all turned to me expectantly, as they invariably do.

"Sorry, lads," I responded to their unasked question. "Things are quiet as a proverbial tomb down in the Detective Bureau today. I hope one of you has something that we can feed to our salivating city editors."

Both Anson Masters, whose beat was the Crime Lab, and Dirk O'Farrell, who had Bunco and Missing Persons, shook their heads. "Okay, I'll bail the lot of you out," sighed Packy Farmer, who covered the Vice Squad. "Thank God you've got me here to save your bacon once more."

"*Once more?* Oh, cut the crap, Packy," O'Farrell snorted. "If we had to rely on you every day, we'd all be out on the street peddling the papers instead of writing for them. "Now just what is it that you have for us?"

Farmer leaned back in his chair, put his feet up on the desk, torched one of his misshaped, hand-rolled cigarettes, and stroked his graying gambler's moustache. "One o' the biggest call-girl busts in the history of this toddlin' town, that's what I've got, boys," he purred, looking at his notes and blowing smoke rings toward the ceiling.

"We await specifics, Packy," Anson Masters rumbled, running a hand over his freckled, bald pate. "And deadlines also await."

"Keep your shirt on, Antsie," Farmer said with a dismissive wave of the hand. "A good story, like fine wine, must not be rushed."

"Okay, Packy, you've had your fun," I barked. "Now cut the horseshit and give us the goods."

Farmer shrugged and favored us with one of his lopsided grins. "Ah, leave it to our good friend Snap Malek to keep us on the straight and narrow," he said. "All right, get your pencils ready. Seems that a very cultured youngish lady, name of Brenda LeBlanc—or so she says—age of thirty-six—also or so she says—has this very chic apartment ten floors up on Lake

Shore Drive overlooking beautiful Belmont Harbor"—he gave us the address—"and that is, shall we say 'headquarters', for a very lucrative pleasure business."

"And just how, pray tell, did our Miss LeBlanc happen to divulge all of this to some of Chicago's finest?" Dirk O'Farrell posed.

"Okay, here's the deal," Farmer said, "It seems that when—"

At that moment my phone jangled and I held up a hand for Packy to pause while I dealt with the call.

"Snap?" It was the familiar, hoarse voice of Murray, the *Trib's* day city editor. "The M.E. wants to see you in his office at ten-thirty. Grab a cab and—yes, you can expense it."

"What's up, Hal? Am I in the soup for some reason or another?"

"Beats me. Maloney doesn't share his thoughts. He just says what he wants."

"Well, I'm right in the middle of getting the dope on this call girl story, and—"

"Let it go for now. You haven't got a deadline for hours. You can pick up on it later. Maloney expects to see you in his office in twenty minutes," Murray barked in his usual machine-gun cadence.

Flagging a Yellow cab on State, I made it to Tribune Tower in eleven minutes and strode into the two-story-high city room— or local room, as the paper likes to call it. J. Loy "Pat" Maloney, the managing editor, was in his glassed-in office on the telephone. He looked up and motioned me in.

"Yes, I understand. Yes, of course, Colonel, we will get right on it," the managing editor said, easing his receiver into his cradle. "That was the man, and he has a story idea," Maloney said, gesturing me toward a chair in front of his desk. He didn't have to explain that he had been talking to Col. Robert R. McCormick, longtime editor, publisher, and principal owner of the *Tribune.*

"Is that why I'm here?"

"Oh, no, no," Maloney responded, tugging on the knot of his plaid necktie. "No, I want to talk to you about another assignment, Mr. Malek."

"Really?" I made no attempt to conceal my surprise.

"You've been at Police Headquarters for a lot of years now, haven't you?"

"Quite a few," I answered, my mouth suddenly dry.

"Quite a few indeed, and you have done a fine job there, yes, a fine job indeed. Including that excitement with President Truman last year.* But everyone needs to stay fresh.

"Just so you're aware," Maloney continued, "we are looking at a lot of our long-time beat reporters with an eye toward making some changes. Good for everyone, you know."

"Just what . . . do you have in mind, sir?"

"You're a darned good feature writer, Mr. Malek. I have read your stuff, of course, and I've also had a lot of confirmation of your writing talent from Mike Kennedy in the Sunday Room, who sings the praises of the magazine-length pieces you've done in the Graphic section on a freelance basis."

I needed a cigarette but didn't light up. "Are you asking me to move to the Sunday Room?"

"No, no, I'm not, Mr. Malek. We are getting ahead of ourselves. As you know, the Chicago Railroad Fair is opening in a few days for its second summer right along the Lakefront. They had such a good year in '48 that they're back for an encore. Sort of like the Century of Progress World's Fair that had its second season in—when was it?—'34.

"Anyway, we'd like you to be our man at the Fair this year. A lot of famous and interesting folks will no doubt pass through it like they did last summer, when we didn't have anyone

---

* See *"A President in Peril,"* a Snap Malek Mystery

permanently assigned there. We missed quite a number of good human-interest stories as a result."

I would be overstating my reaction to say I was in shock, but the truth was that Maloney had set me back on my heels. "Well, this doesn't really sound like my kind of assignment," I said after several seconds of silence.

"Oh, I really don't agree there, Mr. Malek. I've already mentioned the idea to the Colonel, and he was all for it. He's had some very nice things to say about your work over the years."

"How long would this assignment be for?"

"The duration of the fair, of course," Maloney said. "It ends the first week in October."

"Then what? For me, that is?"

"That's a long way off, Mr. Malek," the managing editor said, leaning back in his chair and clasping his hands behind his head. Let's just take things one at a time, shall we?"

"And who, by the way, is going to replace me at headquarters?"

"Westcott. We've already talked to him about the move, and he's enthusiastic."

Ken Westcott currently was a general assignment reporter, not a bad sort, and a fair writer, although he tended to be more than a little lazy. Neither the *Tribune* nor the boys in the headquarters press room would be getting as many stories out of the Detective Bureau as I fed them on a regular basis.

"Is that all?" I asked the managing editor, clearing my throat.

"Yes, Mr. Malek," he said with a smile meant to convey benevolence. "I think this is going to work out very well for all concerned."

I couldn't think of a response, so I got up, nodded, and left his office with my fedora in my hand and my chin bouncing off the floor.

CHAPTER TWO

"Your shoulders seem to be sagging a bit tonight, my love," Catherine said as she embraced me in the living room on my arrival home at our two-story stucco house on Oak Park's Scoville Avenue.

"With good reason, I'm afraid," I told her, setting down my copy of the *Daily News* and taking off my suit coat. "You're looking at a battered old war horse who has just been put out to pasture."

"What in heaven's name are you talking about?" she asked with surprise, backing away and frowning.

We sat side-by-side on the davenport, and I proceeded to tell her about my conversation with Maloney. When I finished giving her the gory details, she cocked an eyebrow as she does when about to make a pronouncement.

"It doesn't sound like you're being put out to pasture at all, darling," she pronounced, caressing my cheek with a slender hand. "This seems like a new challenge, and it could be a lot of fun, too."

"Fun? You call it fun hanging around a bunch of locomotives and train cars and parents with their noisy kids?"

"At the ripe old age of forty-five, you're beginning to sound like a crusty old curmudgeon," she admonished. "And after all, this Railroad Fair only goes for a few months, right?"

"True, but as I told you, Maloney was noncommittal about what would happen in the fall. I have got this uneasy feeling that I'm being eased ever closer to the door, and that the next step after the fair is a pat on the back and a not-so-gentle nudge in the direction of the bread line."

"Why would that be, Steve? You've been a good and loyal employee, and you're an excellent writer. Plus, just a few months ago, you got that bonus from Colonel McCormick himself because of the Truman business."

"Maybe it's the paper's way of saying 'What have you done for us lately?' I don't know, my love. Perhaps I'm being elbowed aside to make way for a younger generation of reporters."

"But there are lots of men at the paper who are older than you. Are *they* being pushed out, too?"

"Not that I'm aware of. Maloney claims the *Trib* is looking at moving other veteran beat reporters to different assignments to 'keep them fresh,' using his words. I think that was really just as a way of softening the blow to me, though."

"Does this Maloney have it in for you?"

I shrugged. "Not that I'm aware of. He's always seemed to be a fair enough joe. Maybe he's getting the word from on high that changes are in order."

"'On high' would mean that Colonel of yours," Catherine said tartly. She is a lifelong Democrat and never has had any use for the resolutely Republican politics of Robert R. McCormick and his resolutely Republican *Tribune*.

"Could be," I answered. "In any case, if I want to continue getting paychecks from the aforementioned Colonel, it appears that my base of operations this summer will be down along our green and well-manicured lakefront."

"I can think of worse places to be this time of year," Catherine remarked, kissing my cheek and easing me to my feet, then propelling me gently toward the kitchen, where dinner awaited.

The next morning, I broke my news to the boys in the Police Headquarters press room.

"What the hell?" spat Dirk O'Farrell. "Doesn't that thick-headed newspaper of yours know that you're needed most right here?" He slapped a palm on his desk for emphasis.

"For once in his long and checkered life, Dirk's right," Packy Farmer put in, gesturing toward his colleague. "It's a gross waste of talent stickin' you out there at that train fair. And then givin' us Westcott, for Christ's sake! That guy filled in once for a couple of days a few years back when you were laid up with the flu or something. We practically had to push him out the door to go and see Fahey. Hell, he even had the gall to suggest that he switch beats with me."

"Which you of course didn't like one bit, Packy," I said. "Anybody who ends up covering the Detective Bureau is actually going to have to put in an honest day's work."

Anson Masters cleared his throat. "Snap, have you informed Mr. Fahey of the impending change?" he rumbled.

"How could I, Antsy? I only walked in the door ten minutes ago, but it will be Subject Number One when I go downstairs for our morning session."

"Speaking of which," Masters said, "it's time for each of us to head for our beats."

Fahey's secretary, Elsie Dugo Cascio, favored me with her usual wide and dimpled grin as I stepped into her closet-sized anteroom.

"Ah, you're looking gorgeous as usual," I told her. "You're the single thing I will miss most about this tired old building."

"Whoa! Stop right where you are, Mister," she ordered, standing and drawing herself up to her full height of five-feet-two—in heels. "Just what do you mean by that?"

"I'll tell you on the way out after I've seen hizzoner the chief. Will you be kind enough to announce me, my dear?"

Elsie threw a reproachful look my way and spoke my name into the intercom, getting a garbled response that I long ago translated as "Send him in."

"Well, Fergus, I have got some bad news for you," I said, flipping a half-full pack of Lucky Strikes onto his desk blotter.

"That's all I need in this job—more bad news," he muttered, crumpling a sheet of paper and dropping it into his wire-mesh wastebasket. "Well, what is it? Don't keep me in suspense."

"Ken Westcott doesn't smoke, as I think that you recall."

Fahey glared at me. "What in hell does that have to do with the price of sirloin?"

"Not a blessed thing, Fergus. But since he's going to be taking my place here, it means you won't be getting free smokes any more."

The chief narrowed his eyes. "You going on a vacation?"

"A very extended vacation, Fergus. Maybe an open-ended one."

His square Irish face registered genuine surprise. "Huh! What the hell, did you get the axe?"

"In a matter of speaking," I said as we both lit up Luckies. I went on to tell him about my new assignment. When I finished giving him the gruesome details, I said that I assumed the department would be staffing the fair.

"We'll have a detail down there like we did last summer," he said. "Standard procedure for big events, you know."

"Was there much trouble last year? As in mischief of an illegal nature?"

He shook his head. "Not much. Oh, there's the usual collection of dips of course. Any time you've got big crowds, you're bound to have pickpockets lurking around the edges looking for easy marks. That's to be expected. It's the same at the ballparks. I can't recall much else that went awry there, though," he added as Elsie waltzed in with a mug of black coffee and set it in front of me on the corner of Fahey's desk.

"Hard to believe you won't be around here any more," the chief said after Elsie left. "I might even miss you."

"I'll try not to get all choked up by all that sentiment, Fergus. You know how I hate scenes."

Fahey leaned back and scowled. "Seems to me, Snap, that wherever you've gone, you've found trouble—or it found you. But I'm damned if I can figure out how you can get into any mischief out there along the lake with all of those choo-choos."

I silently agreed, which goes to show how wrong two supposedly smart gents can be.

CHAPTER THREE

I've never been all that interested in trains, which is why I didn't bother going to the Chicago Railroad Fair in its first summer. Now I've ridden the rails on occasion over the years: to Springfield some years back, for instance, to have a chat with then-State Representative Richard J. Daley; out to various suburbs in search of stories; and when my son Peter was in grade school, we did a one-day round trip to Milwaukee during a phase when he was enamored of the railroads.

When I arrived on the lakefront south of the Loop that sunny June morning to begin my new assignment, I wasn't prepared for the setting. Here was a one-industry exposition masquerading as a world's fair. At that, the masquerade seemed pretty convincing, at least on first glance.

For one thing, this fair occupied roughly the same slender coastal stretch of real estate as an honest-to-goodness world's fair, the Century of Progress, which I had attended fifteen years earlier. My fondest memory of that exposition was meeting and writing a feature about the delightful and coquettish fan dancer, Sally Rand, who had scandalized the more prudish elements of the populace with her so-very-close-to-Lady Godiva-nude-but-not-quite performance. Further, as I got shown around the grounds by Fred Metzger, the public relations flack for the fair, I was struck by other similarities to the '33–'34 extravaganza.

Where the Century of Progress had faux-European enclaves including the Streets of Paris and the Belgian Village, this fair presented such regional American attractions as a New Orleans French Quarter, a Southwestern Indian Pueblo Village, Florida Tropical Gardens, an honest-to-goodness San Francisco cable car operating over a hilly stretch near the lake, and "Gold Gulch," a frontier mining town—each one of them hosted by a railroad that served that particular geographic area. Although all the buildings on the grounds were of a temporary nature and would be dismantled in the autumn, they were designed to look permanent.

"Isn't this great, Mr. Malek?" the ruddy and well-fed Metzger gushed as he steered me through the fifty-odd acres of the fair, pointing out attractions as workers put final coats of paint on buildings and planted palm trees in the Florida exhibit.

"Take this Pueblo, for instance," he said, mopping his brow and indicating the three-story adobe structure. "When the fair opens, we'll have one-hundred-fifty gen-yoo-ine Indians right here, all brought in from Arizona and New Mexico by our good ol' Santa Fe Railway folks. There will be Navahos and Apaches and Hopis and . . . and a bunch of other tribes, too, I forget their names, doing native dances and ceremonies. We're talking actual Indians, yes sir, the real thing, red men from the Southwest.

"Just look at the Pueblo, Mr. Malek," Metzger raved on with the sweep of an arm. "Makes you feel we could be on the Navaho reservation right now."

"Except for *that*," I replied, gesturing toward the shimmering blue, ocean-like expanse of Lake Michigan less than a city block away to the east. "You won't find a body of water like that anywhere in New Mexico. By the way, you can drop the 'Mister' business. I go by 'Snap.'"

"Oh, yeah, somewhere I heard that's what you're called. Mind if I ask you why?"

"Nope. It's because of this," I told him, pointing at the Panama perched on my head. "I'm rarely without one hat or another."

"Oh, now I get it," the PR man said with a giggle. "As in 'snap-brim,' right?"

I nodded and our walking tour continued, Metzger directing me to a large open-air amphitheater along the lakeshore with bleachers seating several thousand facing a wide, paved stage that had railroad tracks imbedded into it. "You were probably here for the fair last year, right, Mr.—er, Snap?"

"Wrong. For one reason or another, I just couldn't seem to make it."

"Really? Well, you're in for a real treat then. A real treat. This is where the 'Wheels-a-Rolling' pageant takes place four times every day. It's a reg'lar history of transportation in the U.S., from the days of the French voyageurs exploring in canoes to the very first trains in the early 1800s to the push west across the prairies and mountains to some of the modern steam and diesel locomotives. There's even some gunfights between the cavalry and train and stagecoach robbers. Exciting stuff. About five-hundred rounds are fired every day. Blanks o'course." Metzger giggled again. The guy was getting on my nerves, but I needed somebody to get me acclimated, and it happened to be him.

"I assume that you worked here last summer, too, right?" I asked.

His smile disappeared. "No, I didn't. The Public relations at the '48 fair was handled by Chester Rawlings."

"Did he retire?"

Metzger shook his head. "No, he had a heart attack, so they say. He was in a State Street subway station and fell onto the tracks in front of a train. It was an awful thing."

"Oh yeah, I do remember reading about it. Tough way to go, although he may have been dead before he hit the tracks."

"I sure hope so," Metzger said. "After that happened, I applied for the position here. I run a little public relations firm in the Loop, just me, one other man, and a girl who answers the phone and such. Plus an intern I've got working for me who you will meet in just a few minutes."

Our tour over, the PR man bestowed upon me a fair press pass in a plastic case that I clipped to the breast pocket of my suit coat. He then showed me to my work space, which was in a windowless room tucked away in the back of the fair's administration building near the 23rd Street main entrance. An unplugged electric fan hugged the floor in one corner. I had a hunch that I'd be using it a lot before the summer was over.

"You've got yourself a desk, a typewriter, and a phone here. All that any good newsman needs, Snap," Metzger said, slapping me on the back.

The drab, plywood-walled room had four other desks, also equipped with phones and no-nonsense Underwood upright typewriters. "Your *Tribune*, bless them, is the only paper that has assigned a man full time to the fair," Metzger told me, bobbing his head in approval as he spoke. "But our understanding is that the other local dailies, and maybe some outlying papers in places like Milwaukee and Aurora and Joliet and Gary will have reporters here from time to time. We hope they will. After all, this is absolutely the closest thing to a world's fair this country's had since before the war. And who knows when—and where— we'll have anything like it again."

Having completed his pronouncement about the gravity of the exposition, Metzger smiled and beckoned me into his small office, which adjoined the makeshift pressroom.

"I'd like to have you meet my right-hand man, Rob Taylor, who's a summer intern on summer break from college," he said heartily, gesturing toward the young man seated at the second, smaller desk in his office. "Rob, say hello to Steve Malek of the *Tribune*."

"Pleased to meet you, Mr. Malek," a boyish-looking young fellow with light blue eyes and a pleasant, guileless face said as he rose to shake my hand with a firm grip.

"Call me Snap, everybody does," I replied. "Where do you go to school?"

"At the University of Wisconsin," he said with a grin, brushing a shock of sandy hair back from his forehead.

"Madison, eh? I was there once, years back. Nice campus, and I seem to remember a lake, right?"

"That's it, a great place, sir—uh, Snap."

"Rob will be doing some of our press releases, and he may be able to suggest some story ideas to you as well. I'm just so glad to have him here," Metzger said, gazing at the young man in what I would call a fatherly way.

"You have an interest in trains?" I asked Rob.

"Not . . . really, but hey, it's a job, right?" the intern said with a marked lack of enthusiasm. When Metzger frowned in his direction, the lad quickly added, "I'm doing my best to learn all I can while I'm here, though."

"Well, I look forward to our working together," I told them both with an upbeat tone that belied my feelings about our being on this strip of land far removed from the pulse of the city.

Back in the press room, I considered my surroundings. As a work space, this was nothing to turn hand springs over. But to give the fair its due, my old spot at Police Headquarters was hardly a paradise, either: a battered desk in a dismal room too cold in winter and too hot in summer, with Elevated trains thundering past the grimy third-floor windows every few minutes. But at least there, I had some company. Plus, for all the internal grumbling I had done over the years about the irritating and eccentric traits of Anson Masters, Packy Farmer, and Dirk O'Farrell, I was already beginning to miss those guys.

My early days at the fair confirmed my initial reservations about the assignment. This was, plain and simple, a featherweight feature assignment. My first byline described the full-blown wedding of a young couple from Central Missouri in the "Fiesta" dining car that served as a restaurant in the Rock Island Lines exhibit.

"We first met on one of them milk runs between Saint Loo and Kansas City," the grinning, freckle-faced groom told me. "When we heard about this fair and this diner, we thought, shucks, lets us go and get married right on a train, see'n as how that's where we came to know each other. And sure enough, my folks and her folks all came up here from Jefferson City, along with some cousins and my honey's ninety-year-old aunt, who'd never in her whole life been out of Missouri, can you believe it?"

I told him that, no, I couldn't believe it in this day and age, or words to that effect. A *Trib* photographer, Phil Muller, took pictures of the wedding party, all of them grinning and squeezed into the narrow confines of the diner, and one of his shots ended up on the photo page of the next day's edition. As he packed up his gear, Muller raised an eyebrow and lowered his voice in my direction.

"Snap, how in the hell did you pull this one off? What a cushy deal you've got here along the lake all day while the rest of us schnooks are at the beck and call of our heartless bosses in Tribune Tower. Just who do you know?"

I answered with a grin and a nod, as if I really were happy to be out here among all the locomotives and Indians and, yes, even palm and orange trees—brought in from Florida and planted by a railroad that serves the Sunshine State. Speaking of Indians, my second fair article was an interview, if you can call it that, with an eighty-five-year-old Navaho who, so I was informed, had never before been off the reservation in New Mexico.

When I asked him about his reactions to Chicago and the fair, I quickly learned that his English vocabulary essentially consisted of "nice place," "big town," and "much water." Somehow, I ground out a ten-inch piece, mostly concentrating on the Navaho's colorful garb and headdress and his lined and classic face, which looked like it should have been in profile on the head of a nickel.

"You are doin' absolutely great out there, Snap. Keep it up," Hal Murray, the day city editor, told me by phone near the end of my first week at the fair.

"That so?" I replied without enthusiasm.

"Hell, yes. That dining car wedding number of yours has drawn all sorts of reaction. At least four people have called in asking how they can get married in the very same diner. And in tomorrow's edition, we're running a letter to the editor from a woman in Elmhurst applauding your piece and complaining that we don't have more 'happy stories' like that one. She writes that, quote, 'Your paper always has too much bad news, not enough good news.' You, Snap, have now officially become our 'good news' reporter," Murray said with a chuckle. "Keep up the great work. I'm sure the Colonel loves it."

My response was a single word—one that the *Tribune* refuses to print.

CHAPTER FOUR

"Well, how goes life at the fair?" Catherine asked as I walked into the house that evening. "Any surprises so far?"

"Not really," I told her, describing my interviews with the young Missouri couple and their wedding and with the taciturn old Navaho. I also told her about Metzger and young Rob Taylor. "Metzger's something of a fussbudget, but the kid seems okay," I said. "Oh, and Hal Murray has informally anointed me the paper's 'good news reporter,'" I told her, grimacing. "Precisely what I've always wanted. From now on, just call me 'Mr. Sunshine.'"

That got a hearty laugh out of her, although she assured me she was laughing with me, not at me.

In addition to the wedding story and the "interview" with the aged Navaho, my first-week file at the fair included a piece on a retired Pennsylvania Railroad engineer named L. J. Gunderson, who was piloting one of the 19th-century antique steam engines that ran on the Deadwood Central western frontier railroad, hauling fair-goers on tracks running along the one-mile north-south length of the grounds.

"This here ain't much of a locomotive, compared to what I'm used to from my days on the grand old Pennsy," he snorted from the cab of his engine, posing for a photo taken by Phil Muller, who seemed to be volunteering for all the fair assignments. "But, pshaw," Gunderson went on, "the folks, especially the kids, in them open-side cars behind me are having themselves such a good time, it just sorta rubs off on me. On top of that, lots of folks want to take my picture, either sitting up in the cab or standing in front of the engine with their kids. Gives a guy a good feeling, you know?"

I told him I knew, and that I was pleased to learn that the old engineer's grandchildren, all four of them, had come in from Valparaiso, Indiana, and ridden on his train just a day earlier.

"Well, they never got to see me at the throttle of the Broadway Limited," he said. When I didn't react, he shook his head in wonderment. "You mean to say you don't know about the Broadway?"

I shrugged my ignorance. "Well, son," he sighed, "it's about as famous as any train in America, and I'm including the Super Chief and the Twentieth Century Limited when I say that. Shoot, the Broadway's the top way to go 'tween Chicago and New York. Best food, best sleeping cars, best doggone crew all the way around. After I retired, my wife and I rode it from here to New York and back. First time I was anyplace besides the engine on that doggone train. Felt like we were royalty, and we got treated like it, too."

I dutifully took notes and tried my best to put on an enthusiastic face. "Must have been great times for you, driving that train," I told Gunderson.

"The very best," he replied with a curt nod. "Got to leave for Gold Gulch now," he said, referring to the reconstructed frontier boom town at the other end of the Deadwood Central line. With two blasts from its whistle, his smoke-belching train eased away from the platform and chugged off, its three cars filled with waving crowds.

After finishing the Gunderson piece and phoning it in to the city desk, I dialed Packy Farmer's number in the Police Head-quarters press room.

"Ah, Snap me fine lad, to what do we owe the pleasure of this call?" he boomed.

"Just checking to see how you reprobates are getting along without me."

He lowered his voice and apparently cupped his hand around the mouthpiece. "Geez, Snap, any way you can get yourself reas-signed back here? Westcott seems to think this assignment is some sort of a walk in the park. Takes two-hour lunches, goes down to see Fahey any old time he feels like it, never mind other people's deadlines."

"Things are tough all over, Packy."

"Not for you. Hell, you're—wait a minute, what am I whis-pering for? Westcott isn't even around. He's on one of those long lunches of his. And I wouldn't be the least bit surprised if he comes back at least slightly looped—again. We're even think-ing of drawing straws to have one of us take over the Detective Bureau beat. *That's* how bad things have gotten."

"That's pretty grim all right," I observed. "One of you might end up having to do some real work."

Farmer snorted. "I can see that I'm not getting any sympa-thy. What did you call for—just to rub it in while you're out there basking along the sun-kissed lakeshore?"

"Sorry, Packy. I really was phoning to see how you guys

were getting along. I'm honestly sorry to hear that Westcott has turned out to be such a dud, although I have to admit that I'm not all that surprised, given some of his past performances as a beat reporter. He should be on general assignment."

"Well, please feel free to have some laughs at our expense, but I've got to believe that sooner or later your bosses up in the mighty Tribune Tower are going to realize what a clinker they've now got on the day shift at 11th and State. I'm making book that you'll be back here with us in the next three months, maybe even sooner."

"Don't bet the farm on it," I told him cheerlessly. "By the way, one of your *Herald-American* colleagues is out here today, Ed Heston by name. Seems that the *Examiner*, your sister Hearst paper out in San Francisco wants a feature done on the cable car and its crew from their burg that's operating at the fair. Heston told me he wished he could be here full time, and I told him that the assignment's overrated."

"Sez you," O'Farrell shot back. "Don't try to kid a kidder. You're lovin' every doggone minute out there, Snap."

I gave him a horse laugh in response and rang off just as Metzger, the fair's public relations man, came into the spartan press room.

"Snap, since you are the only reporter who's here full time, I feel I owe you an early heads-up on something big, really big: Walt Disney is coming to the fair in the next few weeks."

"The man behind Mickey Mouse and Donald Duck, no less? What's his angle?"

"Word we get is that he loves trains, always has. He wants to ride on anything that moves here, even hopes to drive a loco-motive or two. We'll be giving him the red-carpet treatment, of course. I'm planning to send out a general press release when we know the exact dates he'll be here, but I thought that you should know first. You might want to set up an interview in advance for a feature story."

"Thanks, I appreciate that," I told him, although I'm sure that my voice lacked conviction. I knew who Disney was, of course. The whole country did, and much of the world, too, thanks to his comic books and animated films.

Years ago when I was a divorced dad looking for ways to amuse Peter on weekends, we saw "Snow White & the Seven Dwarfs" and "Pinocchio." I enjoyed these movies more than Peter did, though. By that age, he was more interested in things like "Pride of the Yankees" and "Knute Rockne All American." As far as he was concerned, Disney was for little kids, never mind the stunning color and brilliant animation.

Although I didn't share Metzger's excitement about the impending arrival of the famed movie-maker, I knew I would be expected by the editors in the Tower to come up with something about the man who put words in a duck's mouth.

Before I could begin thinking about what approach to take with Disney, Metzger reminded me that he had reserved a front-row seat for me at the afternoon performance of the "Wheels a-Rolling" pageant, which he had been badgering me to see since the day I got to the fair.

"Starts in twenty minutes, Snap. C'mon, let's go. You're really going to love it!"

CHAPTER FIVE

At last, the time is almost here, Papa. It was easier than I thought to get hold of a live round, a real bullet. Now there's one rifle filled with blanks, plus one not-so-blank cartridge. Each of the bandits and guards at the pageant is told to aim his weapon directly at one of the enemy. That way, the stagecoach "robbery" will look realistic, and we have got to please all those thousands of people in the grandstands, don't we? They have paid to see adventure, and . . . well, they're going to get it, all right, maybe in a way they never expected, although the real bullet may never hit anyone, which means I would have to try it again.

I'm more nervous than I thought I would be. But I cannot let the nerves rule me, not now. When I was young, Papa, you always told me to be strong, to suppress my emotions, lest I be seen as weak. When you were young, you had to be strong, I know, even if you never talked to us very much about those rough times.

In the end, here, they broke you, but it was an unfair fight, with small people resorting to small behavior. You were worth any five of them, Papa, and you will be avenged. I am not weak, although others may think so. I am not afraid, although I do feel nervous. But I also feel joy in knowing that I sense that I am closer to you at this moment than I have been in a very long time.

I am thinking of Mama, too, and of the pain she has endured at the hands of the small people.

I wish you could be up in those grandstands today to see just how much your son loves you. My hands are steady now, and I can only hope that the same is true of the one who will fire the weapon that sets in motion our journey of reprisal.

I am no longer nervous now. I feel a calm, a sense of peace . . .

CHAPTER SIX

Metzger led me to a cushioned seat in a cordoned-off section of the first row in the grandstands, roughly the equivalent of the box seats along the third-base line at Wrigley Field. As I sat down, so did he, and I realized that I was going to have the pleasure of his company for the performance.

"I can't get enough of this," the PR man enthused. "This is about the fourth—no, I think the fifth—time I've seen the show. Like I told you before, it's a regular history of transportation in the U.S. I learn something every doggone time I see it." He rubbed his fleshy palms together in what seemed to be a mix of anticipation and nervousness.

"Nice crowd," I said, turning around to eye the multitude in the bleachers that were banked up behind us. "How many does this place seat?"

"Close to five-thousand, so they tell me," Metzger answered. "And it's almost always full, like today."

The stage, if you could so term it, was at least two-hundred feet wide with a concrete floor and, as I had observed earlier, several sets of railroad rails embedded into it. On either side of the broad expanse were high, solid walls that formed the wings. And the backdrop was none other than Lake Michigan, less than a strong-armed outfielder's throw from where I sat.

The stentorian voice of an unseen announcer proclaimed the start of the show. "There was a wilderness to be conquered," he intoned as Indians in full headdress, both walking and on horseback, made their solemn entry. "And the Indians knew these wilds well."

The red men were followed onstage by the buckskin-clad voyageurs, those early French explorers of the Upper Midwest, among them Marquette and Joliet, men who, we were informed in somber tones, "pushed the frontiers ever westward."

So much for the blink-of-an-eye prelude. After all, this was a railroad event, and the pageant's creators lost no time in reminding us of that. We jumped quickly from the 17th to the 19th century, as the earliest steam locomotives, strange-looking contraptions with tall chimneys that I learned were called smokestacks, belched their way onto the stage, spitting out both smoke and steam. They hauled passenger cars resembling stagecoaches, which were filled with stovepipe-hatted men and women in hoop skirts, some of them seated on the roofs of the cars.

I'm no theater critic, so I don't presume to know good staging, but all of this seemed pretty hokey, although it was clear that the effusive Fred Metzger didn't think so. Neither did most of the audience. As I looked over my shoulder into the bleachers above us, I saw mostly animated, happy faces, both adults and children. Mark me down as a curmudgeon, as Catherine has suggested on more than one occasion.

There was a light and humorous moment—supposedly historically accurate—in which one of the early steam engines got challenged to a race against a horse-drawn car on rails. Animal defeated machine by a wide margin, much to the delight of the crowd. But, as we were then informed via loudspeaker, this was but a temporary setback in the railroads' inexorable march to conquer a continent.

Next came the Gold Rush, complete with covered wagons drawn by oxen and men on horseback riding alongside. We were told of the difficulties of these pioneers in their dogged westward movement, and at one point, a young man in suspenders and a broad-brimmed straw hat staggered, keeled over, and lay prone on the ground while a woman wept over his corpse. The dirge-like hymn "Rock of Ages" played as his body was laid in a horse cart that disappeared into the wings.

"Bless him, that chap will be back at the five o'clock show to die all over again," Metzger said with a chuckle. "He's got his role down pat. Isn't this great, Snap? It just gets better as it goes on. I'm tellin' you, you're going to enjoy the whole darn show."

I didn't know it then, of course, but I was never to see the whole darn show.

CHAPTER SEVEN

The pageant continued, with scenes of the Pony Express and of Abraham Lincoln going off from Illinois to Washington as the Civil War loomed. Then, to the tune "O Susanna," a Wells-Fargo stagecoach drawn by four horses careened across the stage as the narrator stressed the importance of this form of transportation on the western frontier before the arrival of the railroads.

We were told, however, that danger lurked, as these coaches frequently carried shipments of gold as well as passengers. On cue, a gang on horseback attacked the stage, rifles blazing. Guards atop the stage stood and fired back and one of them suddenly clutched his stomach, then pitched forward and fell head-first to the ground with a thud that could be heard between gunshots.

"I haven't seen that happen before," a shocked Metzger said as murmurs ran through the crowd.

"And for good reason, I think," I told him as I watched the figure twitching on the concrete. "Unlike that youngster who collapsed next to the covered wagon, chances are this fellow will not be back for the five o'clock performance."

CHAPTER EIGHT

I leapt from my seat and, ignoring the cries of two blue-and-gold-uniformed Andy Frain ushers, sprinted onto the stage and was the first person to reach the man who lay motionless on his back.

"Sir, sir, you can't be out there!" one of the young ushers yelled as I knelt over the prone figure, pressing my fingers against his carotid.

"I'm a newspaper reporter, dammit," I shouted over my shoulder. "Get medical help right now! Get the police!"

Even as I barked orders, though, I knew this man was beyond help. His face froze into a grimace and his open eyes wore the sightless glaze of death. A dark stain had begun to spread over his suede vest, and his forehead sported an eggplant-colored bruise where he had hit the pavement.

For those first few moments, I was only vaguely conscious of the growing intensity of the crowd noise and the stares from members of the suddenly shocked troupe, who looked down from their horses and from the stagecoach. One of the "bandits," rifle in hand, began to sob, perhaps in the realization that he may have fired the fatal shot.

Siren wailing, an ambulance screeched onto the stage, lurching to a stop as two white-jacketed medics jumped out. I stepped away and backed into the crowd of gapers who had edged onto the stage despite the efforts of the beleaguered ushers to keep them back.

A pair of uniformed policemen arrived and had better success in keeping the onlookers at bay. "What's going on here?" one asked hoarsely after I had identified myself.

"Guy was shot," I told him. "Fell from the top of a stagecoach."

The cop's ruddy Irish face registered outrage. "Holy Mary, Mother of God, there's way more guns bein' used in this show than is necessary; I said so right from the start to anyone who would take the time to listen to me," he snarled. "Too easy to have a live round get mixed in with the blanks when you've got this much ammo to play with."

"So you think this was an accident?" I asked the cop.

"Of course it was an accident!" Fred Metzger sputtered as he tried to get between me and the patrolman, whose nametag read "O'Brien." The PR man panted, beads of sweat materializing across his forehead. "You don't have to write about this, do you?" he pleaded, arms outstretched.

"You darned well know the answer to that!" I snapped at him. "First thing I need is an ID on the poor bastard."

"You wouldn't be tryin' to get in our way now, would you?" Officer O'Brien asked, puffing out his already ample chest.

"Not at all. Just doing my job, same as you. Are more of your men on the way?"

"Yeah, some dicks will be here soon enough," the burly copper said, shaking his head in disgust. "And they'll want to be talking to all the actors in this cussed show. Christ almighty, I figured this was going to be an easy detail, like it was last summer. Now don't you go quoting me on that," he quickly added.

"I won't, don't worry. I've got other things on my mind, and so do you." By this time, the two medics, although out of earshot, had made it clear by their actions that there was nothing more to be done. As they covered the body with a sheet, the loudspeaker crackled, "Ladies and gentleman, boys and girls, because of an unfortunate accident, this presentation of 'Wheels-a-Rolling' has been cut short. However, there will be two more performances today. Thank you, and enjoy your time at the Chicago Railroad Fair."

As the crowd descended silently and somberly from of the grandstands, many of them cast furtive, almost guilty glances at the grim tableau of the medics loading the body into the ambulance and driving off. Several of the actors, still in costume, gathered in small groups on the stage talking in hushed tones. I joined one group of three young men in their twenties wearing Stetson hats, Levi's, buckskin vests, cowboy boots, and chaps and introduced myself as a *Tribune* reporter, flashing my press card.

"Did any of you know the . . . uh, victim?" I asked them, glancing from face to face.

"A little bit. Yeah," the one with a goatee muttered, looking down and scuffing his boot on the concrete.

"What can you tell me about him?"

"Name is—was—Vic. Never knew the last name."

"I did, it's Trevor," said the tallest of the three. "We were both in the same small theater company up on the North Side. Trying to get a foothold into the business, you know?"

"We're all actors—or attempting to be," the third guy added sheepishly. He wore an eye patch that turned out to be a prop.

"Would you say you know most of the other performers in this pageant?" I posed, directing the question at all three.

"Not really," the bearded one said. "At least I don't. Oh, I've talked to a few of them backstage, mostly idle chatter. Some of the older ones are retired railroad workers. Others just like being on the stage. For instance, I met one woman who's in the Harvey Girls scene, has three kids, and lives up in one of the northern suburbs, Northbrook, I think it is. Used to act in community theater groups before she became a mom."

"Harvey Girls?"

"You know, those girls who have worked in Santa Fe railroad station restaurants in the Southwest since way back when."

"Guess that was going to come later in the show, right?"

"Oh—yeah. We didn't get that far today. You haven't seen the show before, huh?"

"No. You know anything more about this Trevor?" I asked.

"Came from someplace in Minnesota or maybe Wisconsin," said the tall one. "I only talked to him a few times, but I think he had a small apartment up in Lakeview or maybe it was Rogers Park."

"Do you have any idea how long he had been in Chicago?"

"I couldn't say for sure. At least six or more months, though. We were in a play together in January at a small theater, which was the first time I saw him."

"Any of you know anything about the guy who fired the shot at him?"

The all shook their heads. "I was riding inside the stagecoach with three others," Eye Patch said, "and never saw what happened."

"And I was up on the roof with Vic, but I was facing the other way firing my rifle when he got . . . you know," the tall one put in.

"And me, I was driving that darn coach," added the goateed lad. "Never knew what happened till I got a jab in the ribs from the guy riding shotgun next to me, who pointed down at—what was his name . . . Vic?"

I thanked all three and scribbled their names in my notebook as Officer O'Brien came over to us. "We're askin' all of you who had a role in the pageant to stay here until the detectives have had a chance to talk to you," he said, addressing the three and then going off and telling other actors to hang around for questioning.

I then looked up to see two plainclothes men on the far side of the stage talking to another of the actors—the shooter. I walked over and introduced myself to them.

"We're sort of busy right now," one of the dicks snapped at me. "Oh . . . I remember you now. Yeah, Smart Aleck Malek, isn't it? Kindly don't bother reminding me that you're a buddy of Chief Fahey. I've heard that crap from you before. It didn't cut any ice then, and it won't now. Why don't you just beat it, scandal-monger?"

It was none other than Detective Jack Prentiss, who I'd had a run-in with before. He didn't like reporters, which made us even, because I didn't like him. But you've got to pick your fights, and this was not the time. I retreated to a spot several yards away and watched as Prentiss and his partner, whom I didn't recognize, questioned the shaken young man who still gripped the fatal rifle.

Every so often, Prentiss glared in my direction, as if willing me to disappear. It didn't work. After about fifteen minutes of conversation, in which both detectives scribbled notes, they started to walk away, taking the rifle with them.

"Pardon me, gentlemen, but I'd like a couple of minutes of your time," I said to the pair, pulling out my own notebook.

"I thought I told you before to beat it," Prentiss snarled, "and I meant it, Malek. Since you're such a buddy of the chief's, go and talk to him. You have an in there, as you've told me. We got work to do here, people to talk to. Lots of people." His partner graced me with a sneer similar to Prentiss's. They must practice it in detectives' school.

The young man had headed quickly into the wings after his talk with the detectives, and I sprinted until I caught up with him, immediately identifying myself as a *Trib* reporter.

"Go 'way. Don't wanna talk to anybody," he muttered, head down. Like the others I had spoken to, he was lean and dressed in western garb and looked to be in his early-to-mid twenties.

"I'll just take a couple of minutes," I said. "I know this is a tough time for you. Those cops didn't charge you with anything, did they?"

He shook his head, tears welling in his eyes.

"I didn't think so. No reason they should. Any idea how your rifle happened to have a live round in it? Or was it more than one round?"

"No idea, mister. Look, I already told those policemen everything I know. And they told me make sure to stay around here where I can be reached, for an inquest or something like that. I got nothing more to say to anybody."

"Well, it's important that we make our readers—by far the largest audience in the Chicago area—aware of your story. Otherwise, well . . . people might always wonder . . ."

It was clear that he was wavering, so I pushed on. "Look. I'm giving you a chance to tell your story to more than a million people. They need to know that you are completely without blame in this terrible tragedy. I'm here to help you. You can see that, can't you?"

He stared down at his boots and nodded, jamming his hands into the pockets of his Levi's and sniffling.

"Okay, good. First, tell me your name and how you came to be part of this pageant."

"It's . . . Todd Forrest."

"How old are you, Todd?"

"Twenty-three. I'm a part-time waiter at a little café up on Belmont near Halsted. I'm trying to break in as an actor, like a lot of the others in the cast here. I answered an ad for a part in this . . . show, and got cast as one of the stagecoach robbers."

"Uh-huh. Where are you from?"

"River town out in Iowa, Muscatine. You've probably never heard of it."

"There's a lot of places I've never heard of, but that doesn't make them bad. Have you been in Chicago long?"

"'Bout two years now, ever since . . . ever since I graduated from the University of Iowa."

"I've heard all sorts of good things about that school. So, you auditioned for a role in the pageant, right?"

He finally looked up and made eye contact. "Yeah, I did."

"Any particular reason that you got picked to be a bandit?"

Todd took a deep breath. "I'm . . . fairly good with guns. Used to go duck-hunting a lot with my dad along the Mississippi River as a kid. They—the people who did the casting for the pageant—liked that. They wanted at least some of us to look like we knew how to handle firearms, although we all were told to aim at the other guys to make it look realistic. Some of 'em just fired into the air, though."

I nodded as I continued taking notes. "So, Todd, exactly where did you get that rifle you used today?" I asked.

"Same place as always. At the start of every performance, each of us gets issued a replica of the Sharps 44-caliber rifles that they say were used on the frontier back on the 1800s. There are six blanks in each weapon. And we fire all of them during the attack on the stagecoach. The men riding on the stagecoach do the same."

"Who passes out the guns?"

"Guys on the backstage crew. Then they—the rifles—get collected after our act."

"How many of these guys are there?"

"I dunno, two or three, I guess. I never paid much attention to them."

"Who loads the rifles?"

"Afraid that I couldn't tell you. Maybe the same crew that gives them out."

"Do you always get the same rifle?"

He shook his head. "Naw. The guys passing them out don't even bother to look at us. We just line up and get handed a weapon. They usually don't say a word, except maybe 'here you are, buddy' or something like that."

"Do you have any idea how many of your shells were live?"

Todd began tearing up again. "Only one, I think, although 'course I didn't know it at the time. Live rounds have a slightly different sound and a stronger recoil, too. Wish I wasn't such a good shot. As I said, a lot of the actors just fire without aiming."

"Did you know the one who. . . ?"

"Only to say hi to. I didn't even know his name. This was only his third or fourth performance. People are changing all the time in the cast. Some get moved to other acts in the pageant, depending on if anybody's sick or something. Others quit if they land a role in some local play. God, this is awful."

"On that we're agreed, Todd," I said putting a hand on his shoulder. "A photographer for the paper may be taking your picture."

"Well, I'm not going to be around here all that much longer," he said in a listless tone. "After I get done testifying, or whatever it is that I have to do, I'm getting a one-way ticket back home to Muscatine. You can have this darn city of yours. I don't care if I never see it again."

CHAPTER NINE

The shot was on the mark, Papa, and I know that it caused a death. One might say the man who died was innocent, but no more innocent than you were, so I feel no remorse, none whatever. I realize for the first time that this is only the beginning. Now others will be sacrificed to atone for your suffering. I have been waiting so long for this opportunity, and at last that wait is over. Rejoice with me . . .

CHAPTER TEN

My phone jangled as I strode into the fair's empty press room. I had an idea who was calling, and I was right.

"Snap, we're getting word there's been a fatal at the fair, a shooting," rasped Hal Murray on the city desk against a backdrop of clattering typewriters and nattering voices. "But no details yet from Westcott at Headquarters. We need something for the early edition. Where in the hell have you been? This is my third call."

"Covering said fatal, Hal. I was about to phone in an eyewitness report."

"From who?" he yelled.

"It's *whom*. And from me, of course; who d'ya think? I saw it happen, talked to the shooter, even got insulted by a police detective. All in a day's work," I said, sighing for effect. "Now how 'bout giving me a rewrite man?"

I spent the next fifteen minutes dictating copy, good copy, to Williamson. "No quotes from the cops?" he drawled after I'd finished.

"The dicks out here weren't exactly in a talkative mood, Eddie, although one patrolman did complain that there are too many guns out here. I gather Westcott still hasn't called in from 11th and State."

"Not far as I know, Snap."

"Well, maybe he'll weigh in with comments from Chicago's Finest. Also, the chances are that you'll be hearing from me again."

I dialed a number that had been burned into my brain years ago. "Chief Fahey's office," Elsie Dugo Cascio chirped.

"Is our noble leader available, you vision of loveliness?"

"Be still, my heart. It's a voice from the past, come back to haunt me and invade my dreams. As a matter of fact, he just mentioned your very name a few minutes ago. I will put you through."

"Dammit man, does trouble just follow you around, or do you follow it? I've never figured that one out," Fahey growled.

"And a good afternoon to you, too, Chief Fahey. I had the displeasure earlier this very today of running into that lout Prentiss of yours. You ought to send the bastard to charm school. That is, if they offer remedial courses. He's at the kindergarten level."

"Okay, okay, I already know how you feel about Jack," he said with a sigh. "Now tell me what—." He was stopped in mid-sentence by a buzzing sound that I took to be Elsie with another call.

"Gotta go," he barked when he came back on the line. "Your Mr. Westcott is here to see me. Can't keep the *Tribune* waiting, right?"

"Absolutely, I—"

"Give me your number there. I want to talk to you after I get done answering your colleague's incisive questions."

Twenty minutes later, my desk phone rang. It was Fahey.

"Westcott tells me you already phoned in a story including some quotes from the shooter. Mind sharing those quotes with me?"

"Not at all, but don't you trust your attack dog Prentiss to be thorough in his own questioning?"

"No comment. Besides, I haven't heard from him yet. And from what Westcott also told me, you were an eyewitness. I'd like your slant on this, if it's not too much trouble."

"Okay, Fergus, that's fair enough." I gave him my account of the shooting as well as a verbatim on the conversation with Todd Forrest.

"Bizarre," Fahey muttered when I'd finished.

"True. Might have been an accident, a live shell somehow finding its way into the shipment of blanks. Could have happened at the factory or arsenal or wherever this stuff gets made."

"Maybe," the old copper said. "But as you know, I'm suspicious by nature. Our next move is to talk to whomever the people at the fair are who load those miserable rifles."

"Mind if I sit in on those talks?"

A snort. "You know that's impossible."

"Well, you can't blame an old newshound for trying. After all, you should be willing to give a little quid pro quo. I've already thrown some information your way. And I can be an extra pair of eyes and ears for you out here. You know that I'm dependable."

"I know I can depend on you to find trouble—usually for yourself. "The answer is still no, Snap. There still are such things as regulations and procedures, as you are well aware."

"Okay, I surrender—but only up to a point. How about telling me what your men find out after they've talked to the rifle-loaders?"

"Shouldn't I be sharing that with your Mr. Westcott here in the building?"

"No reason that you can't tell us both, is there?"

"I guess not," the chief conceded. "Besides, it might get you off my back, although that may be too much to hope for."

"Probably. By the way, for what it's worth, I think the kid who did the shooting is clean. Call it a reporter's intuition."

"No reason to doubt it—yet," he said. "But even if he is clean, I've got myself one doozie of a headache on my hands."

"Why? There's no way in the world I can see how the department could have prevented this."

"Huh! Just try telling that to the editorial writers on your paper and those other rags you compete with. They'll all find ways to blame us. Just watch. 'Insufficient monitoring of dangerous materials, etc., etc.' The commissioner is already bouncing off the walls. He's going to be all over me."

"I thought you and Prendergast got along pretty well."

"We do, that's never been a problem," Fahey said. "But he's going to be feeling the heat, and when he feels it, I feel it. After all, we've got ourselves a shooting death at the city's major summertime event. An event, not incidentally, that brings in hundreds of thousands of visitors who leave behind hundreds of thousands of dollars at such places as hotels and restaurants and nightclubs. And also don't forget the taxi drivers and souvenir shops and tour buses and how much they make on all these additional visitors who flock to our fine metropolis.

"The folks who run the exhibition are having a goddamned conniption, to say nothing of all the railroad presidents who've put up the dough to sponsor this fair. They'll be demanding that we double or triple the size of our detail at the fairgrounds. Never mind that we're already stretched thin all across town, thanks to a local government that won't give us more men. That's all off the record, of course. So much for my two-week July escape to the calm and cool of Wisconsin."

"You would miss the excitement of the city," I countered lamely.

"Try me, just try me. All hell's going to break loose around here."

Fahey had it right. The next day, each of the four papers led with the shooting, and my first-person piece drew the *Tribune's* banner headline: GUN DEATH AT RAIL FAIR. Also, all four dailies, per the chief's prediction, carried editorials demanding both an immediate investigation and increased police presence at the fair. The *Herald-American*, true to its Hearst roots, ran its editorial in a box out on Page One under the headline ARE WE SAFE ANYWHERE? The answer, according to the editorial, was a resounding "no!"

When I arrived in the fair's press room the morning after the shooting, I found reporters already there from the *Daily News* and the *Sun-Times*. "To what do we owe this honor?" I asked the two, both of whom I had crossed paths with on occasion over the years.

"You know goddamn well, Malek," said raw-boned, lantern-jawed Dave Stapleton of the *News*, who'd been with the paper as a crime reporter at least as long as I had worked for the *Trib*. Despite all those years he had been in Chicago, he still spoke with a voice that gave away his Texas roots. He lit a Chesterfield and sat on one corner of the desk that had a DAILY NEWS sign taped to it. "Understand you saw the shooting here yesterday."

"Yeah, Snap, give us the rundown," put in the blocky, cigar-chomping Chick Cavanaugh of the *Sun-Times*, who had started out on the predecessor tabloid *Times* in the late '20s and had covered the St. Valentine's Day massacre up on Clark Street, as he was quick to tell anyone he met.

"It was all in my story this morning, lads, assuming that you took the time to read it."

"Ah, I see that we're full of ourselves today after getting the line story in the God-almighty *Tribune*," Stapleton said, cocking his head and flicking ashes from his cigarette onto the wood-plank floor.

"For the record, I've gotten lots of line stories," I told him, yawning.

"Don't go acting smug just because your fat, rich paper can afford to keep a man out here full time and the rest of us can't," Cavanaugh huffed.

"Now calm down, both of you," I said. "For old times' sake, although I don't recall any old times to speak of with either of you, I'll recap what I saw here yesterday, and then you're on your own."

They pulled out their reporter's notebooks and scribbled as I recounted the events at the pageant. I was just finishing when Fred Metzger walked into the pressroom.

"Ah, Mr. Stapleton, Mr. Cavanaugh, I see you picked up your press credentials at the front gate," he said, gesturing toward the badges they wore. "Wonderful to have you here," he exuded, mopping his brow with a well-stained handkerchief. "You can help keep Mr. Malek company. Now, can I give you both a tour of the grounds?"

"Speaking for myself, just the place where the shooting happened," Stapleton snapped. "I don't know about Chick here, but I also need to talk to the guy who fired the rifle."

"Oh, I'm afraid I can't help you there," Metzger said with a frown and a shake of the head that made his jowls jiggle. "He's, well . . . he's not available, as I understand it. I believe he has left the acting troupe here. I assumed you both had come to cover the grand scope and color of the fair and—"

"Oh, cut the crap, flack," Cavanaugh snarled. "My paper leaves that kind of fluff to our nice lady feature writers, people like, well . . . like Malek here." He sent a sneer my way, but before he took another breath, I yanked the cigar out of his yap and ground it under my heel.

"Next time, you overstuffed tub of lard, I'll turn that nickel stogie around and jam it down your throat ash-end first," I hissed, looking down at him and giving his wrinkled tie such a yank that he almost toppled over forward. "Got it?"

"Gentlemen, gentlemen!" Metzger whined. "Please, there is no need to get belligerent. We're all here to do honor and justice to the fair."

"Maybe *you* are," Stapleton drawled to the PR man. "Me, I'm here looking for a story, and frankly, I don't give two horned owl hoots about whether what I find does justice and honor to the fair or not. You're paid to be a flack, I'm sure as hell not. Sorry to put it so starkly, but that's the way things are, like it or lump it."

"I'll second that," Cavanaugh said, looking at me reproachfully as he straightened his tie and tried without success to square his rounded shoulders. "Somebody got himself shot dead here, and that makes it news. More news by far than anything else that's going on around this train carnival."

"Even though it was just an accident?" Metzger asked in a querulous tone.

"Just who says it was an accident?" Stapleton fired back, crossing his arms over his chest. "Hey Malek, has anybody talked to the people who loaded those doggone rifles?"

"I haven't got the foggiest idea, Dave," I told him. "As your loud-mouthed, sawed-off crony here from the *Sun-Times* said,

I'm just a feature writer now. Why bother asking me anything?" They'd gotten enough information from me for one day. Let them burn up some shoe leather.

"You wouldn't be jiving us now, would you?" Stapleton answered, eyes narrowed. "Once a police reporter, always a police reporter, I say."

"That so? Well, I'll think about those words while I'm interviewing one of the long-legged lassies who water ski at that Cypress Gardens Water Show out in the lake. But then, that wouldn't interest either of you hard-bitten, toughguy crime chasers. Gotta run boys."

In fact, I *did* interview one of the nubile blonde lovelies in the water show, which was a copy of the original version in Florida and had been underwritten by one of the railroads that transport Chicagoans south to the warm weather come wintertime. Sure enough, none other than Phil Muller showed up to take the photos, and he took plenty of them—far more than necessary.

As for the young lady, one Melissa Sue Harkness, age nineteen, of Dothan, Alabama, she didn't have a lot to say, other than that she was "honored to be chosen for this wonderful opportunity to present our show to the wonderful people of Chicago and all the other visitors to the fair," a phrase she used three times in a voice that could melt ice cubes while they were still in the refrigerator.

I dutifully filed a few paragraphs, knowing full well that my words would play second-fiddle to one of Muller's cheesecake shots, which the picture editor, himself a lover of the feminine form, probably would spread across at least three columns.

That chore completed, I wandered through the crowded fairgrounds, looking for feature material. So far, I had got a few story suggestions from the paper, but I'd done each of them—including the water-skiing belle—and no further inspiration was forthcoming from the Tower, although Metzger had proved to be a decent source of ideas.

My wristwatch told me it was just about time to knock off for the day, so I vowed to come in fresh in the morning, filled with ideas. As it would turn out, a story was to present itself, but not the kind I expected.

CHAPTER ELEVEN

The time has come yet again, Papa. This will be different from the last one, and I will do my best to make sure that very little pain is felt. I have not become an avenger simply to inflict hurt, but to carry out the necessary work quickly and efficiently. The real pain, mental rather than physical, will be keenly felt by those in charge here, the ones who care only about themselves, their precious companies, and their pocketbooks—not about the many who toil with loyalty and diligence so that their leaders can enjoy the spoils.

I think of you every day of my life, Papa, and I will continue to until the very last, when I lie down to die . . .

CHAPTER TWELVE

Figuring I needed time to noodle on story ideas, I got to the fair earlier than usual the next morning—8:20 by my dependable Elgin watch. I had just settled in at the desk when an excited Rob Taylor, Metzger's summer intern, dashed into the PR man's office, panting.

Metzger quickly closed his door, but through the plywood wall I could catch snatches of the young man's excited conversation: ". . . on the ground . . . first thing this morning . . . just lying there . . . awful, awful!"

I'd heard enough and barged into the little office. "What's going on?"

Metzger was flustered and swallowed hard, looking at his intern. "Rob here says he was over at the . . . the New Orleans French Quarter, and there's—"

"There's a body on the ground there, and, and . . ." Rob sputtered, waving his arms.

"Let's go right now!" I barked.

"Wait," Metzger said. "We need to—"

"You can come or not, but I'm on my way," I shouted over my shoulder. The New Orleans exhibit was only a few hundred yards away, and after a three-minute trot, I found myself in the square that had been made to look like a slice of that tourist city's French Quarter.

A cluster of people had gathered at a decorative fountain in the center of the plaza. I elbowed my way through the small crowd and spotted the object of their attention.

On the pavement next to the ornate fountain lay a thin, gray-haired man in a red shirt and long white waiter's apron. His tongue protruded and his sightless eyes stared skyward. His slack mouth was open. The cause of death seemed apparent: A knotted loop of twine embedded in his thin neck. I had seen enough corpses over the years to know that the guy had been dead for hours.

"Who is this?" I barked above the sobbing of a hefty woman in braided hair and an apron who knelt beside the body.

"George Burnwell," said an ashen-faced old fellow beside me who looked like he might keel over any second. "Like me, he is—was—a waiter at the Café St. Louis." He tilted his head toward an archway that led, I knew, to a train dining car that adjoined the street scene as part of the Illinois Central Railroad's elaborate exhibit.

"Has anybody called the police?" I asked, looking around at the grim faces.

"We all just got here to open up for the day," said a woman in a ruffled blouse and a red hoop skirt. "When we came in, we found . . ." She sniffled and gestured toward the body.

At that moment, one of Chicago's Finest barreled into the courtyard, out of breath and followed by an equally puffing Fred

Metzger. It was the very same uniformed cop, O'Brien, who had arrived on the scene shortly after the stagecoach shooting.

"All right, all right, don't anybody leave here," he ordered. "There's detectives on the way who'll want to talk to all of you. Who found him?"

"Actually, several of us did, sir," the hoop-skirted woman volunteered. "We all arrived at just about the same time."

"Now ain't that just convenient, though!" he snarled, hands on hips.

"But, don't you see, it's the same each day," she insisted. "We are told to be here at 8:30, which gives us an hour to get everything set up, what with the gates opening at 9:30 and all."

"Well, he musta got here first today," Officer O'Brien said, shaking his head and looking down at the body.

"More likely, he never left last night," pronounced the old waiter next to me, who had somewhat composed himself. "George, he was in charge of the dining car, like in the old days on the I.C. when we both worked as stewards running those grand diners on the Panama Limited and the City of New Orleans. In a restaurant, you would have called us maitre d's. Every night here, he stayed around to tidy up after the rest of us went home. He was a real perfectionist. Everything had to be just so."

"Well, then he must have—" O'Brien halted in mid-sentence as two square-jawed, grim-faced plainclothes dicks in fedoras strode up. I was pleased to note that neither of them was Jack Prentiss.

The senior man of the pair, who identified himself as Corcoran, swiftly took over. "I'm going to want to talk to everybody here, one by one. Someplace private we can go?"

"Detective, I'm Fred Metzger, in charge of public relations at the fair. My office is close by, or if you prefer, we can use the dining car that's part of this exhibit. I'm sure that the Illinois Central folks won't mind."

"But, we're opening to the public in a little while to serve brunch," a tall, dark-haired fellow in a business suit said plaintively.

"The diner sounds fine to me. You'll just have to open up later than usual today," Corcoran replied crisply. "Murder trumps everything else."

With that, the detective and his partner led the gathering through an archway between the quaint stuccoed buildings and toward the dining car. I turned in the opposite direction, heading for the press room and a telephone.

"Hey you, where you going'?" barked Corcoran's sidekick, who I later learned was named Baxter.

"I'm a *Tribune* reporter. Hafta file a story. I'll check in with you later."

"Get back here!" he bellowed, but I had already left New Orleans.

"What in God's name is going on at that fair, Malek?" Hal Murray on the city desk demanded in his usual machine-gun cadence after I had given him a quick rundown from my desk in the empty press room.

"Like Chief Fahey has been saying for years, trouble just follows me. I'll give rewrite a few graphs for the two-star, then I've got to get back and see how the cops are doing." I proceeded to dictate the bare essentials, including the dead man's name. Seconds after I'd hung up, the phone rang. It was Fahey.

"I just got word about this latest—" He uttered one of those words that the *Tribune* will not print. "Fill me in."

"Isn't that what you have a whole regiment of men for? To fill you in?"

"Yeah, but I like to hear what you think, too."

"I'm honored, Fergus, I really am. I haven't got a lot for you, I'm afraid, but I did get to the scene a little ahead of the uniformed man and your guys."

"Why am I not surprised?"

"Anyway, as we speak, Detective Corcoran is interviewing people over at the Illinois Central exhibit, where it happened, along with his sidekick."

"That would be Baxter."

"Okay. I've never met either of them. Anyway, it seems that the victim, old fellow, name of Burnwell, was garroted sometime last night, probably as he was closing up. You probably already know that."

"Sort of, yeah. Give me your take."

"Eh . . . I don't have one. The guy was a retired railroad employee. Used to work in the dining cars, for what that's worth." Fahey spat a *Tribune* no-no word again.

"Yeah, it's one hell of a mess, all right," I sympathized. "I'd better get back there. Baxter was sore when I broke from the group gathered around the body to call the paper. Before I go, anything new to tell me about the earlier mishap?"

A snarl came over the wire. "Things are pretty casual at that fair of yours," Fahey said, "and the employees, if you can call them that, seem to drift in and out like day laborers. "There were three men who loaded blanks into the rifles at the pageant every day, and one of them didn't bother showing up again after the shooting. He had filled out an employment card when they hired him, but the address he put down on North Clarendon doesn't exist. For that matter, he probably doesn't exist either, at least under the name he put down."

"Which was?"

"White, Samuel White. On top of that, the Social Security number he put down also is a phony. I already gave all this to your replacement, of course, and presumably, he passed it along to those other leeches up in the press room."

"Did the guys who White worked with give you a description of him?"

"Yeah, I also fed that to your replacement."

"How 'bout feeding it to me, too? After all, I'm still on the *Trib* payroll."

Fahey made a production of growling.

"Come on, Fergus, humor an old friend."

"Seems that I've been humoring you for years now. I've come to feel like it's part of my job description. Okay, according to his fellow rifle-loaders, he was pretty ordinary. Somewhere in his mid-forties, about five-ten, brown hair, mustache, mole on his right cheek. He talked with what was described as some sort of a slight foreign accent, although they weren't sure what it was—possibly German or Swedish."

"And that's it?"

"That's it. Now you know what we know about him."

"All right, thanks. I'll be talking to you, Fergus."

"That's what I'm afraid of. Each time we speak, I get a new headache."

"Take two aspirin and call me in the morning," I told him, hanging up before he could mount a retort.

CHAPTER THIRTEEN

When I returned to the Illinois Central exhibit, I found several people clustered around the door to the dining car. Officer O'Brien stood just outside their little circle, making sure that nobody drifted away as I had earlier.

"Hey, you were here before, right after they found Burnwell," said a little guy with a mustache and a flat cap. "That one cop wearing a suit was doggone mad when you left."

"Well, I'm back now. I'm a *Tribune* reporter, and I needed to phone my office."

"About this?"

"Yeah. What's going on inside?" I asked, gesturing toward the dining car.

"They're interviewing all of us, one at a time," said the woman in the hoop skirt. "I don't know of anything we can tell them that will help."

"They have to go through the motions, though," I told her. "Did any of you know Mr. Burnwell very well?"

The old fellow, whose first name was Orrin, spoke up. "Like I said before, George and I used to be in charge of dining cars on this line before we retired. He was always a hard worker and took his job very seriously."

"Did George make any enemies along the way?" I asked.

Orrin lifted his shoulders and let them drop. "Not that I know of. Oh, I suppose some of the dining car staff might have got upset with him from time to time. He was a taskmaster, but then, so was I," he added proudly. "And I don't think that I ever made what you could call enemies."

"Anybody else here have something to add about him?" I asked, looking around the somber little group. They all shook their heads.

"I really didn't know him well," a small woman put in, "but he seemed very nice. I'm a waitress in the diner, and he was always gentlemanly, both to the staff and the customers. There aren't enough men around like that anymore." She began sniffling and pulled a lacy handkerchief out of a lacy sleeve, dabbing at her face.

"Was George always the last one to leave here at night?"

"Oh, yes, yes sir," Orrin said, nodding. "He was a widower, didn't have anybody to go home to, and he said being here beat sitting around in an empty apartment."

"Where did he live?"

"Out south, around 71st and Jeffrey Boulevard. He laughed about how he'd worked for the Illinois Central for forty years, and now he was commuting up here to the fair on the same darn railroad. He just couldn't get away from the ol' I.C., he liked to joke."

"Uh-huh. Did he work at the fair last year, too?"

"Yessir, and so did I. We had a lot of fun serving in the diner. It was like the old days, when we was still working, and we even got a little bit of money for it, too." Orrin looked down at his polished shoes and shook his head.

"Did he have any children?"

"None I was aware of, no sir. He was all alone in the world."

Just then, Detective Baxter opened the door of the diner and eyed our gathering at the bottom of the steps. "Okay, who's next? Anyone?"

Nobody seemed anxious to get grilled, so I volunteered, climbing into the brown-orange-and-yellow streamlined railway car.

"You!" Baxter spat. "The reporter, right?"

"Guilty as charged," I said with a grin. "You wanted me back here, so I'm back."

He made a face and led me into the dining car, with its white linens and silver and a rose in a slim vase at every table, all ready for customers. At a table for four in the middle of the car sat Detective Charles Corcoran, shuffling through papers, presumably notes that he had taken.

He looked up at me without enthusiasm. "*Tribune* man, huh?"

I nodded, sliding into a chair across from him. A stony Baxter remained standing, arms folded across his chest.

"I'll be honest, Mr. . . . ?"

"Malek."

"I'll be honest, Mr. Malek; I have never been a big fan of newspapermen."

"Sorry to hear that."

"I doubt it. Anyway, that's neither here nor there at the moment. Tell me, how did you happen to be at the scene—and so quickly?"

I filled him in on my ongoing assignment at the fair and my learning of what had just occurred at the New Orleans exhibit.

Corcoran still wore the dubious expression. "So you must have been around when that guy got plugged at the pageant, huh?"

"Yes, I happened to be in the audience."

"I read the report on that business," the detective said. "I seem to recall that Detective Prentiss mentioned your name in it."

"That so?"

"Yeah. Somehow, I got the impression he wasn't happy to see you on the scene."

I leaned back and fired up a Lucky Strike. "I couldn't say. Maybe like you, he doesn't care for newspaper reporters."

Corcoran wrinkled his brow. "Didn't you used to work at 11th and State?"

"That's right."

"Does that mean that you're in thick with Chief Fahey?"

"I know him, which isn't surprising after all these years. I'm hardly in thick with him, though," I said, brushing the question away with a hand.

The cop exhaled and looked at his notebook. "All right, as a reporter, you're supposed to be observant. Give me your impression of the scene when you arrived this morning."

"I must have gotten there five—maybe ten—minutes after the first ones on the job had found the body. I'm no expert, but it was obvious that Burnwell had been dead for hours. He was awful to look at."

"All stiffs are. Any of the people who were standing around act funny?"

"My impression was that most of them were pretty shaken. They seemed to like the guy."

"That's all?"

"Yes, why? Have any of the people you talked to acted suspicious?"

"I'm the one asking the questions here," Corcoran shot back as if he were starring in a grade-B crime film.

"Fine by me," I said offhandedly. I already was on the shit list of one detective, Prentiss. No sense alienating a second.

"Okay, Malek, you can go," Corcoran said curtly, glaring at me.

I rose and walked down the aisle of the dining car toward the door. My back was turned to Baxter, but I would have laid odds that he was glaring, too.

CHAPTER FOURTEEN

It was over so quickly, Papa—in just seconds, so it seemed. I am sure he felt almost no pain, and he did not struggle to speak of. He was old, and would have died soon, anyway. I admit to feeling nervous at first, never having killed with my own hands before. But then, just before it happened, I became very calm. My hands are still shaking a little now, although I know that soon will pass. However the panic here on the fairgrounds will not pass, but rather grow, as I continue to seek a peace for you that never came when you were alive.

Now I shall begin to plan my next action. If all goes well, I believe it will occur in, of all places, a tunnel—and not a tunnel of love. Oh, I know that I should not joke about such things. There is nothing whatever here to laugh about. Believe me, Papa, I am as serious as I have ever been in my life . . .

CHAPTER FIFTEEN

"Oh, Steve, not another death at that fair," Catherine said as I walked into the house after work and we embraced in the living room. "It was on the radio. What's going on? I thought that of all places, you had a nice, safe assignment there."

"It certainly figured to be," I agreed. "But at least your husband is getting himself some scoops, which didn't happen all that often at Police Headquarters, what with its share-and-share-alike policy."

"And your wife is getting more gray hairs," she said glumly, passing a palm across her temple.

"Might I remind you, my dearest, that you were reared in a newspaper household. Your Daddy, whom I had the privilege of meeting on several occasions, was absolutely fearless, a real bulldog of a street-smart reporter. Not afraid of anybody."

"Yes, but Mother and I worried about him, just like I worry about you. A small-time hoodlum named Kelso once threatened to kill Daddy because of some of the things he wrote. He might have, too, if he hadn't got shot himself by some other mobster a few weeks after he had made the threat."

"Well, at least you had some idea of what you were getting into when you married me," I said lightly, pressing her to me and kissing her thick, wavy, and not-at-all-gray hair. "I assumed that you were drawn to my exciting, swashbuckling style as an intrepid reporter for a great metropolitan newspaper."

"Not just a *great* newspaper, 'The World's Greatest Newspaper,'" she said, mocking the *Tribune's* self-proclamation, which ran each day on Page 1, just below the Gothic-style nameplate.

"Okay, so maybe that's just a little bit too presumptuous," I conceded. "But then, newspapers have never been known for their modesty. *The New York Times* has a box on Page One every day that reads: 'All the News That's Fit to Print.'"

"True, newspapers are not modest by nature. Nor newspapermen, for that matter," she said, at last allowing herself a smile. "Are you ready for dinner?"

"Those were the words I was waiting for."

As we ate pork chops, baked potatoes, and green beans, I filled her in on the day's adventure, including my semi-contentious dining car meeting with Detective Corcoran.

"Steve, is it true that most policeman dislike reporters?" she posed. "I can't remember if I ever asked Daddy that question."

"Not really. Sometimes they actually curry favor with us because they like to see their names in print. Part of the problem comes when the editorial writers blast what they view as police inaction or corruption. Sometimes these attacks are deserved, sometimes they're not.

"But when this happens, the cops, including the ones on the beat, transfer their anger to anybody who happens to work for the newspaper. Then, because reporters are the ones on the paper who interact the most with the police, they—we—are usually the ones who end up feeling the wrath."

"What about you and that other detective you've told me about a few times?"

"You mean Jack Prentiss?"

"Yes, that's the man."

I leaned back, dabbed my mouth with the napkin, and patted my satisfied stomach. "This may come as a surprise to you, but your loving husband is not perfect."

She put down her fork as if shocked. "Fascinating, tell me more."

"This Prentiss, he's surly by nature, but I have to take some of the blame here. It dates back to Pilsen, and my cousin Charlie's apartment. You remember that awful night when I drove over there and everything that happened."

"I'll never forget it."

"Well, what I probably didn't tell you, I can't remember for sure, is that when I met Prentiss there in the apartment, I made sure he knew that I was close to Fergus Fahey, his boss."

She leaned forward, resting her elbows on the table. "No, I don't think you ever mentioned that."

"That was a stupid, arrogant move on my part. It was like rubbing his nose in the fact that I could go over his head any time I felt like it. He has never forgotten about it and probably never will."

"Well, you certainly seem to get along well with Chief Fahey."

"That wasn't always the case. When I first got assigned to Police Headquarters way back when, I was a real smart-mouth, and it didn't sit well with him. Over the years, I like to think I've mellowed at least somewhat. It took awhile for things to thaw between me and Fergus, but now, yeah, I think we get along fine, given our respective roles; we understand each other. For instance, if he tells me something is off-the-record, I honor that."

"Isn't that the, well . . . *honorable* thing to do, though?" Catherine posed between sips of her coffee.

"Yeah, but it's the practical thing to do as well, honey. He knows I'll keep my word on stuff he's not ready to break; in return, though, I get the news first when he is ready."

"But then you have to share whatever you get with your so-called competitors in the press room."

"True, that's the unfortunate part of being one of the Headquarters press crew. It's always share and share alike. The damned system is as old as the hills."

"Well, as you know, I've never thought much of that practice. Now, as to these deaths at the fair, do you think that they are connected?"

"I don't see how, unless this 'mystery man' who was one of the rifle loaders also strangled that poor old bird last night in what passes for Chicago's version of New Orleans."

"The rifle loader who then disappeared," Catherine said.

"Right. That would be the non-existent Mr. Samuel White of a non-existent address up north on Clarendon Avenue."

"How in the world are the police going to find him?"

"Beats me. That's Fahey's problem. I'm sure his men have questioned everybody on the fair crew who worked with or around the so-called Mr. White. From the description I got, it sounds like other than a slight accent, which isn't all that uncommon in Chicago, he could blend into a crowd of three. Although, although . . ."

"Although *what*, Mr. Steve Malek? When you get that look, I start to worry. This is a police matter, plain and simple. Just stay out of it!"

"Is that an order?"

"As if I could ever order you to do anything," she said with an exaggerated pout.

"Now you know that's not true. Just last night, you ordered me to take out the garbage, and I did."

"That was not an order," she said, leaning across the table and punching me lightly on the shoulder. "That was a strong suggestion. And now I have another one. I'll wash and you dry."

"Sounds like a good plan," I said, glad that the conversation had drifted away from the man known as Sam White.

CHAPTER SIXTEEN

As was the case when I'd toiled at Police Headquarters, I got Saturdays and Sundays off from covering the Railroad Fair. This weekend, Peter was coming over to the house with his fiancée, Amanda Rogers. He and I would make our annual pilgrimage to Wrigley Field for a Cubs game Saturday, then the four of us would have dinner in the stucco house on Scoville Avenue.

Catherine had met Amanda for the first time just a month earlier when we went down to Champaign for Peter's graduation from the University of Illinois Architecture School, and the two had quickly hit it off. The weekend had been an interesting one, to say the least. My ex-wife, Norma, came down to the ceremonies with her husband, Martin Baer, and Amanda's parents had driven over from St. Louis to see their daughter graduate with a degree in art history.

After the young couple had been awarded their diplomas, the eight of us had dinner together at a steak house near the campus in Urbana. I had not been looking forward to that gathering, given that whenever I had been around the successful and polished haberdasher Baer, it was a reminder of my own past failures as a husband. But the evening turned out surprisingly well, largely because of Catherine.

She appeared totally at ease, even though this was the first time she had met either Norma or her husband. She also was animated and radiant, and any residual envy I felt toward Baer completely dissipated, never to return. So you might say it was a pivotal moment in my life.

It also helped that Catherine and Amanda, seated side-by-side at dinner, chattered on like two old friends who hadn't seen each other for ages. When, two weeks later, Peter had call to tell us that he and Amanda were engaged, Catherine clapped her hands and actually squealed—something out of character for my normally reserved wife.

"Steve, she is perfect for Peter, just perfect. I was hoping for this!" I whole-heartedly agreed with her judgment. She then suggested we have them over for dinner, and I concurred again.

They came to the house at ten that Saturday morning, giving Peter and me plenty of time to get up to Wrigley Field. The women, meanwhile, were going into Downtown Oak Park to shop. "It's a nice town." Catherine told Amanda as they tripped out the door, "although I'm afraid you will find that our Marshall Field's store is tiny compared to the one down on state Street in the Loop."

"Hey, I'm really happy for you," I told Peter as we rode a Lake Street Elevated train into Downtown Chicago, where we would change to a northbound train. "In a span of just a few weeks, you get yourself a degree, a good job in Downtown Chicago, and a wife. I call that a true triple play!"

"Thanks, Dad. I'm a little worried about the job, though."

"How so? It's supposed to be one of the biggest, best architectural firms in town, and maybe in the whole country, for that matter. Haven't your first few weeks there been good?"

He nodded, although he was frowning. "Yes, things seem to have gone fine, and everybody's been nice to me. It's just that the place is loaded with talented people. These guys have designed skyscrapers, hotels, art museums, hospitals, stadiums, schools, even a cathedral up in Canada. I'm not sure that I'll ever be in that league. I feel like going around the office asking for everybody's autograph. These are many of the same people that I've been reading about for years in magazines like *Architectural Forum* and *Architectural Record*. One of my professors in school even had us analyze a Boston office building that was designed by one of the partners."

"All of these big names had to start out somewhere, though," I put in.

"True, although somehow, Peter Malek doesn't sound very impressive. No offense meant about our name, Dad."

"None taken. But that's it—of course! Those grand architects with their multiple names: Frank Lloyd Wright, Edward Durell Stone, Ludwig Mies van der Rohe. Well, you can be Peter Reed Malek." Reed is Norma's maiden name.

"It sounds a little ostentatious," Peter said with a laugh.

"Maybe, but that's how your birth certificate reads. Anyway, it's something to think about down the road, when you become famous."

"If and when I ever do become famous, I'll give you all the credit, Dad. After all, you got me that summer job with Mr. Wright himself."

"Yes, but you worked hard out there in the wilds of Wisconsin and made the great man sit up and take notice."

"Thanks. Now I need to have the folks at my new job sit up and take notice."

"They will, I am absolutely convinced of it. Now, if we can just convince the Cubs they're not a last-place team," I said as our northbound El train pulled into the Wrigley Field stop, Addison Street.

But alas, the Cubs showed once again why they were mired in eighth place as they lost to the Phillies, 4–3. Because the game the day before had been rained out, the teams played a double-header that Saturday, but rather than be late for dinner at home, we skipped the second game. It was just as well, because Philadelphia flattened the bumbling Cubs in that one, 9–1.

Prime rib is not normally on the menu at our house, but Catherine made an exception that balmy July night. "After all," she had told me earlier in the week, "it isn't every day that your son brings a fiancée home for dinner."

The talk at the dining room table ranged from how bad the Cubs were—they would indeed finish in last place at season's end for the second straight year—to the quality of the stores in Oak Park—"excellent," Amanda proclaimed—to the Railroad Fair.

"So Dad, now tell us about these murders," Peter asked as we finished the apple pie ala mode and sipped coffee.

"I'm still not sure the shooting really was a murder," I said. "Although after the strangling, you have to wonder what's going on."

"Let's talk about something a little less . . . unpleasant at the table," Catherine suggested. "By the way, Steve, have you noticed Amanda's ring?"

"Yes, I have. It's a real beauty," I said as the girl held out her hand and smiled.

"We have you to thank," Peter told me, coloring slightly.

"Oh? And why might that be?" Catherine asked, wearing a puzzled expression.

"Well . . . Dad advanced me some money," he said sheepishly. "But he'll get it back soon, now that I'm drawing a paycheck."

"Why, you sneaky old romantic," Catherine gibed at me. "I had no idea that you had stepped up. Not that I would have objected." She turned to Amanda. "How are the wedding plans coming along?"

"Pretty well," she said. "As you know, the date is set—second Saturday in October. Our minister back home in Missouri is all lined up, and my parents plan to have the ceremony and reception at home. In the back yard, if the weather cooperates."

"They've got a really nice house," Peter added. "It's big enough that they could have the shindig inside if they had to."

"The only thing that would keep me away from said shindig is if the Cubs happen to be in the World Series that week," I announced. That was good for a hearty laugh all around the table.

"Are you having any luck as far as finding a place to live?" Catherine asked Amanda.

"We've been looking at apartments mostly up in the Lakeview and Rogers Park neighborhoods," she said. "We'd like to find a building close to one of the stations along the Howard Elevated line. That way, the train would drop Peter just a couple of blocks from his office in the Loop, and it would be just as handy for me, too, assuming of course that I'm able to get the job that I've applied for down at the Art Institute."

"Which is?" I asked.

"An assistant to the curator of 19th Century European Art. That was my area of concentration in college. Please, all of you keep your fingers crossed for me."

"Amanda's a cinch for the position," Peter put in. "They would be foolish to miss out on all of her expertise."

"You are absolutely right, sir," I added. "If she doesn't get the job, I promise to use every ounce of my influence at the *Tribune* to urge its readers in an editorial to boycott the museum."

"You wouldn't really, would you?" Amanda said, eyes wide.

"Of course he wouldn't, even if he could," Catherine sniffed, brushing the idea aside with a hand. "You have to learn to believe somewhere between one-third and one-half of everything he says."

"Well, it's moot anyway," I stated, "because she will be hired, there's no question about it. You all heard it here first."

Let the record show that it was less than a week later when Amanda received a phone call from the Art Institute telling her to report for work on the following Monday.

CHAPTER SEVENTEEN

I got to the press room at the fair Monday morning at the same time as Fred Metzger. "Any problems here over the weekend?" I asked the PR man.

"Just more police and more newspapermen tromping around all over the place," he groused, waving his arms in frustration. "One of the officers told me they were going to add several men to the detail here. I asked that they be in plainclothes so as not to worry the visitors. Do you know what he told me?"

I shook my head.

"He said it's important that the police presence is obvious, so as to discourage troublemakers. I argued, but it didn't do any good."

"For what it's worth, I think the badge you talked to is absolutely right. Instead of worrying visitors, the sight of more uniformed figures would be comforting to them."

Metzger looked unconvinced, then shrugged, turned on his heel, and walked out onto the fairgrounds, presumably to glare at some cops. A couple of minutes later, the intern, Rob Taylor, walked by and gave me a wave on his way to the PR office.

"You just missed your boss," I told him. "He's in a funk over all the cops that are crawling around the grounds."

He laughed. "Yeah, he told me he thinks it will scare people to see so many of them. To me, it seems like it's a good idea, though."

"On that we agree, Rob. By the way, how'd you happen to land this job?" I asked.

"You sound like you're interviewing me for a story," he said in a voice that bordered on accusatory.

"Sorry, I didn't mean to. An old reporter's habit, I suppose. Hard to break."

"That's okay," he said, blushing slightly. "I didn't mean to be so defensive. As to how I got the job, I called the fair office from up at school back in the winter," he said. "I told them I was looking for work as a summer intern doing public relations—I've taken some courses in advertising, which is sort of related. Anyway, they told me that Mr. Metzger was going to be doing the PR, and they gave me his number."

"That's pretty enterprising of you."

He hunched his shoulders self-consciously. "They tell us at school to take the initiative when we're looking for work. At first, Mr. Metzger didn't sound interested, but I told him I'd be willing to work for very little money. I wanted the experience."

"You live in Chicago? Whoops, there I go again, playing interviewer."

"South Side, with my mother," he said.

"Well, I'm sure you are plenty of help to your boss here. And we'll be seeing a lot of each other."

"If I can help in any way, I'll be glad to, sir," he said.

"Remember, it's Snap."

"Uh . . . Snap, right," he said with a sheepish smile, turning toward the PR office.

After Rob left, I sat at my desk and dialed a number.

The "hello" on the other end was fuzzy, as I had expected.

"Hello yourself, you old rascal. Are you keeping out of trouble?"

"Is this who I think it is?" muttered "Pickles" Podgorny.

"I dunno, I'll play the game. Who do you think it is?"

"Listen, typewriter jockey, haven't I told you many times before that you are never, ever to bother me before 1 in the afternoon. I work nights, as you are very well aware."

"Yes, and I also know exactly what kind of work you do. The only blisters that you'll ever get in your so-called labors are on the fingertips of your dealing hand."

"Have you called just to make sport of a tired old man?"

"No, although you are one tempting target. Truth to tell, I'm phoning with a hard-to-refuse offer to buy you lunch."

"Uh-oh, why do I suddenly feel like this lunch is somehow going to cost me?"

"Don't be such a cynic, Pickles."

"Any cynicism that I might happen to have comes from knowing you for lo these many years. What's the deal?"

"I'll tell you over lunch."

"At that same old joint over on Wabash, the one near Headquarters?"

"Oh, no, sorry. I'm assigned to the Railroad Fair this summer, and—"

"Ah, you mean the place where they're dying right and left?"

"As usual, Pickles, you exaggerate."

"Maybe, but it doesn't seem like the safest spot in town these days." He groaned. "All right, where should I meet you?"

"The Fiesta dining car, at the Rock Island Railroad exhibit. It's a nice clean place, white tablecloths, hearty sandwiches—and they even come with pickles, kosher dills. See you at noon."

"You mean I'm going to have to pay to get into that blasted fair?"

"I will reimburse you the princely admission fee, and the cab fare too, for that matter. How's that for a deal?"

"You're all heart, Snap. Although it's against my principles to take nourishment that early in the day, I'll see you at noon—or close to it."

In fact, it was 10 past 12 when Pickles Podgorny peered suspiciously into the Fiesta dining car from the door at one end. I waved him to my table.

For those of you new to these narratives, Pickles is a Chicago fixture—as a former bookie and two-bit grifter, and, in his current line of work, a far-better-than-average poker player. Early in his checkered career, he ran afoul of the local gendarmes, mainly because of some small-time cons he was running. I met him more than a decade ago when he got himself pinched for operating a crap game in the back of a saloon only two blocks from Police Headquarters.

Curious about what kind of guy would be nervy enough to rattle the dice right under the noses of the law, I went to his court hearing, wrote a feature about him (which never ran), and hooked him up with a lawyer who got him off with little more than a slap on the wrist and a stern lecture from the judge.

As a result, Pickles, who now confines his gambling to poker, felt a certain debt to me—a debt I have cashed in on numerous times by taking advantage of the man's vast knowledge of the cast of characters who inhabit the city's seamy underbelly. In fairness, I have paid him for his knowledge and information, as I once again was prepared to do.

An unshaven Pickles, all five-feet-seven of him, slid into the chair opposite me and took off his flat cap, slapping it down on the starched white tablecloth. "Helluva place to get to, this fair," he grumbled, scratching a nose that was too big for his face. "I never knew there were so many people who liked trains. Can't see the attraction myself."

"Well, thanks for coming at what for you is an ungodly hour. Let us order, then I'll tell you a story. By the way, as I mentioned on the phone, they have excellent dill pickles, and I'm willing to bet the waitress will give you an extra one if you ask her nicely."

We ate our ham sandwiches in silence, and Pickles did indeed get an extra dill, which, given his nickname, is a high priority. Over coffee, he squinted at me, scowling. "All right, Mister Deadline-a-Minute, let's get to it. What's the angle?"

"Ah, Pickles, I trust that you enjoyed your corned beef on rye?"

"Not bad. You know, when you told me on the horn that you're working out here now, I suddenly put two and two together, even in the haze of just waking up far too soon. I read the papers. I know there've been a couple of stiffs here the last few days, and I sez to myself, 'Now just why would my old buddy Snap Malek be calling me out of the blue? Could it just maybe have something to do with one guy getting shot and another guy getting strangled?'"

"You are indeed a perceptive man, Pickles. I have often said so."

"Yeah, perceptive happens to be my middle name. So what?"

"So, I'm looking for a man."

"Would the police also be looking for said individual?"

I nodded, sipping coffee. "You read the papers, so you know at least something about the shooting at the pageant here."

"I know a little, but I have got this feeling you're going to tell me more."

"I am. As you are aware, somebody put a live round in among the blank cartridges in one of the rifles used in the stagecoach robbery at the pageant they stage here several times a day."

"Could have been an accident."

"Could have, but you don't believe that for a minute!" I snapped.

Pickles grinned. "'Course not. I just wanted to get a rise out of you. It worked."

"Okay, score one for Chicago's reigning king of five-card stud. Three men had the job of loading the rifles before each show."

"Let me guess. Right after the shooting, at least one of the guys lammed, not to be seen again."

"Bingo. And that's precisely where you come into the story."

"Not so fast, wordsmith. It'll take more than a free lunch, taxi money, and an admission ticket to this here fair to compensate for my valuable time."

"Okay, you chiseler, here's a double sawbuck on top of what I already gave you for the round trip in a cab," I said, pulling a twenty from my wallet and setting it on the table in front of him. "Now can we continue talking?"

He looked at the currency, sniffed, and pocketed it. "You know I'm worth more than that, but what the hell. For old times' sake . . ."

"Old times' sake, my ass. You haven't done a thing yet, and you're twenty bucks ahead, plus a fat sandwich and two juicy kosher dills."

"The pickles were all right," he conceded grudgingly.

"Glad to hear it. Now, here's the description of the missing rifle loader: "Thought to be in his mid-forties, white, about five-ten, sandy hair, mustache, mole on his right cheek."

"Well, that narrows it to about a hundred thousand men in town." Pickles grumped.

"And he talks with what was described as a slight foreign accent."

"What kind?"

"Nobody seemed sure. Maybe German, maybe Swedish, maybe Dutch."

"Oh, swell, that narrows it to maybe fifty thousand. Does this bird happen to have a name?"

"Samuel White is what he put down on his employment form at the fair."

"Geez, Snap, that's just Jake. Why didn't he call himself John Doe and be done with it? Talk about the old needle in a haystack! This is ridiculous. I suppose you're going to tell me he gave a phony address when he applied?"

"I am. A number up on Clarendon that doesn't exist. Also, the Social Security number he gave was bogus, too."

He rolled his eyes. "Isn't that just peachy now?"

"Pickles, if it was anybody but you, I would agree the job is well-nigh impossible, but given your special talents—"

"What special talents would those be?"

"Your, shall we say . . . *knowledge* of the activities of certain persons who don't want the knowledge of their activities made public."

"Meaning, of course, hoodlums, miscreants, lowlifes, grifters, and various others that your esteemed journal might call 'the dregs of society.'"

"Well put, sir. I could not have said it better myself."

"Of course you couldn't. Did you by chance talk to the guy who fired that live round?"

"I did, and I'm convinced he's totally clean. I believe the cops are convinced as well. He's a young actor trying to make it in town."

"Okay, now what about the poor sap who cashed in?"

"Pickles, I have to believe it was totally random. He was a fellow in his early twenties from up in Wisconsin, an actor trying to break in as well."

"So, how do you see all of this tying into the second death?"

"It might just be a coincidence, but almost surely isn't."

"Could it be somebody with a grudge against that railroad line whose exhibit was where the second murder took place?" Pickles asked as we got coffee refills.

"The Illinois Central? That might explain the strangulation, but not the shooting. There was no connection in that particular pageant act to any one rail line."

"Back on the subject of this elusive Mr. White: Any idea how he happened to get hired by the fair in the first place?"

"Nope. But if I were to guess, I'd say he answered an ad in one of the papers. I know the fair did some advertising for a lot of positions."

"Do you know if the cops have checked on all those outfits that hire day laborers?"

"I couldn't say."

Pickles slapped his forehead with a palm. "You're not a heck of a lot of help, do you know that?"

I spread my hands. "Regard this as a challenge, as well as an opportunity to make the cops look bad. I know just how much you'd relish doing that."

"The problem is that even if I do make monkeys out of them, they'll never know it was me. I'm not about to do anything that calls attention to yours truly. I've had too many dealings in my previous life with what some of us laughingly refer to as 'Chicago's Finest.'"

"But Pickles, think of the personal satisfaction you'll get if you do finger the elusive Mr. White. Isn't that worth something to you?"

The answer I got was a scowl, followed by a glare, followed by a word that was mouthed silently, in deference to the families with children who were seated near us in the crowded and festive dining car.

CHAPTER EIGHTEEN

The next several days at the fair were uneventful, the highlight, if you can call it that, being my interview with a cowboy in the rodeo show put on by a group of western railways. Fred Metzger told me this Montana-born cowpoke was some kind of champion bronco buster who had won awards at events like the Calgary Stampede and the Cheyenne Frontier Days. That may well be, but he had about as much to say as the old Indian from the reservation whom I had talked to my first day on the job at the fair.

This sample from the interview is all that you need:

ME: So, tell me what it takes to be a top bronco buster.

COWBOY: Ya gotta show 'em who's the boss, ya know? That's the secret, right there.

ME: How do you do that?

COWBOY: By letting 'em know right from the start, yes sir, right from the very doggone start, that you're in charge.

ME: Do you talk to them? Do you do something else to establish control?

COWBOY: It's the way ya mount 'em, the way ya ride 'em, that lets 'em know that they can't mess with ya.

ME: Can you describe that?

COWBOY: Now that's real hard to say. But you know what I mean. All ya gotta do is watch me.

In fact, I didn't know what he meant, and I knew even less when, an hour after we had talked, he got thrown over the head of a bronco after being on him for less than a few heartbeats.

I had a feature story to file, though, and I tried to make the best of it, describing the cowpoke as "a lean, leathery, raw-boned son of the rugged Montana mountains and plains, a man of few words in the finest tradition of such taciturn cinematic Western heroes as John Wayne, Gary Cooper, and Randolph Scott."

I went on to depict the rodeo itself and "the cheering young-sters in the stands who squealed with delight as they watched the riders desperately try to stay on their angry, snorting, wildly bucking charges." I made no mention, however, of my subject's embarrassingly short ride that day. Who am I to let specifics get in the way of a good story?

As the week wore on, it became obvious that the police presence had intensified throughout the fairgrounds. A lot of uniforms were in evidence, as well as several men in suits whom I recognized to be plainclothes detectives. I even spot-ted Jack Prentiss himself once, and we looked daggers at each other, reflecting our mutual distaste, although no words got exchanged.

One morning I called Fergus Fahey. "Don't you have enough to do out there on the lakefront without harassing me?" the chief snarled.

"Hey, I'm not harassing you, I'm just keeping in touch

with an old friend. I didn't want you to think I'd forgotten all about you."

"I should be so fortunate."

"But I thought that maybe you missed our daily conversations. I do."

"Snap, don't beat around the bush with me. I know you too well. You just want to learn what we've found out about the deaths out there."

"Well, now that you mention it . . ."

"Isn't it enough that I keep your man Westcott briefed every day?"

"How's he doing, by the way?"

"No comment."

"That bad, huh? I'm really sorry to hear that, Fergus, but it would not hurt you to fill me in, too. After all, I can be a real asset to you out here, another set of eyes and ears."

"Your allegiance is to your paper, not to the police department," he said dryly.

"And your allegiance is to the department, not to any of the papers, mine included. That doesn't mean we can't help each other."

He exhaled into the receiver. "Not much to report. We've talked again to that young actor who pulled the trigger, and it seems obvious that he's clean. As for the two rifle loaders still on the job, they swear they only put blank cartridges into the weapons. And neither one of them knew the third one, White— or so he called himself. They said in the few days they all had worked together, he didn't say anything about himself except that he originally came from someplace in Europe, although he wasn't specific. He never mentioned where he lived in Chicago, or whether he had a family. They said he was one very close-mouthed customer."

"And your men have checked out all the Samuel Whites in the phone book, I suppose?"

"You suppose right," he muttered. "For the record, there are seven in all, none living on Clarendon, and every last one of them got a visit from us. Two are Negroes, which lets them out. And not one of the other five speaks with anything resembling even a slight foreign accent. Also, all but one is employed and can account for their time on the day of the shooting. The other is seventy-seven years old and has been retired since before the war. Oh, and the suburban directories got checked, too. Three more Samuel Whites, none with an accent. There, have I now filled you in enough?"

"On that particular situation, yes. What about the strangling?"

"Dammit, Snap, I can't spend all day talking to you, not the way things are crashing down around us here. If you haven't noticed, the heat is on the department to make your cursed train fair as safe as all that gold stored underground at Fort Knox."

"Nothing on the strangling then?" I persisted.

"No! We've interviewed everybody we could find who knew the dead waiter—neighbors, former co-workers on the railroad, even members of his Baptist church in the South Shore neighborhood. Nobody—not one single soul—had anything bad to say about the man. He apparently had no enemies, no debts, no affairs with married women, no apparent vices such as gambling or whoring. Now if you'll excuse me, Elsie just walked into my office and help us a sheet of paper that says Commissioner Prendergast wants to talk to me. He's under the gun, which of course means that I am, too. Looks like we'll have to face an inquisition from your colleagues in the news business." Before I could respond, the line went dead.

The next day's papers all had pieces on a press conference in which Prendergast, Fahey, and Mayor Martin Kennelly reiterated the city's commitment to keep the Railroad Fair safe, and the mayor insisted that the two deaths on the grounds were merely an aberration. Unfortunately, violence at the exposition was about to become less an aberration, more a common occurrence.

CHAPTER NINETEEN

Thursday dawned clear and fresh, one of those precious July mornings that make Chicagoans forget for awhile the miseries of a long and dreary winter. I rode into the city on a swaying Lake Street Elevated train whose windows were open and whose passengers seemed by outward appearance to be uniformly at peace with the world. The same was true on my streetcar ride south from the Loop to the fairgrounds.

On both legs of the trek, I alternated between reading the *Tribune* and planning my day at the fair. Through Fred Metzger, I had lined up an interview with the governor of Washington State, who was coming to the fair under the auspices of the Great Northern Railway to promote his corner of the continent as a vacation destination—one that was easily and comfortably accessible by Great Northern trains, of course. My questions to him would include whether the rainy climate in Seattle and its environs depressed its populace, or whether what we in the rest of the country had heard and read was an unfair depiction of a vibrant city in a picturesque setting.

My spirits dampened the instant I entered the press room at the fair. A uniformed and grim-faced police sergeant was just leaving Metzger's office.

"What's going on?" I asked as I walked into his sanctum and saw the rotund flack slouched behind his desk, looking like a man whose sure-thing horse had just finished last at Sportsmen's Park.

"Another death," he moaned. "This one in the Moffat Tunnel."

It took me a few seconds to realize what he was talking about. As I had learned early on at the fair, the Denver & Rio Grande Western Railroad had built a truncated replica of the historic tunnel as part of its exhibit. They had hauled in tons of boulders and created a miniature "mountain" with a tunnel in it and an arched stone portal that mimicked the real one at one opening of the six-mile-long rail passageway that burrowed deep beneath the Colorado Rockies.

"My God, what's the story on this one?" I asked the deflated press agent.

He shook his head, eyes glazed, and slouched even lower into his chair. "A man who works as a movie projectionist in the little theater the Rio Grande operates at the end of its tunnel was found lying dead in the tunnel this morning. He must have had a heart attack, from the looks of it."

"Well, at least it wasn't violence," I said by way of trying to soothe him. It didn't help.

"What difference?" he moaned, throwing up his hands and letting them drop limply into his lap. "It's still news for you and for everybody else. It will be in all the papers and on the radio and even on the television now, for those who have sets."

"I certainly can't argue that. Well, I'd better get over to the exhibit." But before I could leave the building, I heard my desk phone ringing.

"Malek? We're just getting word of yet another stiff out at your choo-choo fair!" It was Hal Murray on the city desk.

"Just heard about it myself. I'm headed that way now."

"Shake a leg, will ya, Snap? I'm gonna need some on-the-scene stuff for the two-star. Thank God we've got you out there."

"Yeah, thank God indeed," I muttered. "Like I've been saying for years, what would all of you do without me?" I didn't wait for his reply, cradling the phone and sprinting out.

Five minutes later, I arrived at the realistic (I assumed) mock-up of the Moffat Tunnel portal. Two uniformed coppers and a like number of detectives formed a circle around a body that lay on a railroad track just inside the tunnel. Several other people formed a larger arc around them, all looking on in a stunned, respectful silence.

I edged through the outer ring and identified myself to one of the plainclothesmen, who was kneeling next to the corpse, a stocky, bespectacled man who looked to be somewhere in his sixties. The hatless dick and his partner were both new to me. Fergus Fahey apparently was rotating his men at the fair, which was fine by me as long as Jack Prentiss got rotated out permanently. This probably was too much to hope for.

"How long has he been dead?" I asked the kneeler, a burly specimen in a blond crew cut.

"Dunno," he snapped. "Medic's on the way and can give us an idea."

"I found him right there, around eight, already dead," a man in a security guard's uniform put in. "His face was blue and his lips was kinda purple-like. And he had a little foam around the mouth. Ticker musta gave out on him."

"We don't know that!" the crew cut dick snapped. "Let's not go jumping to conclusions until we have all of the facts, huh?"

"Who is he?" I asked, turning my head to take in the whole gathering.

"Jack Openshaw, John technically," answered a short, skinny fellow wearing a trim gray mustache and a badge that proclaimed that he was a Rio Grande guide. "I take people through the tunnel, explaining how it was built and giving them all sorts of statistics on its cost, length, and so on. You'd be surprised how interested folks are.

"As you can see, the tunnel isn't very long, just enough to give folks an idea what the real one's like inside," continued the guide, who clearly liked to hear his voice. "The track is just there to make it more realistic. Nothing runs on it. At the far end down there we've got a little movie theater where we play a film about our line, the Denver & Rio Grande Western, and all that great part of the country where we operate. Jack, he is . . . he was our projectionist."

I nodded. "Think he could have been lying here since last night?"

"Not that it's any of your business, but I've already asked that," the detective snarled, looking fiercely up at me from his crouch. "Just who's running things around here, the Chicago Police Department or some self-important newspaperman?" He mouthed the last word as if it were contagious.

"Sorry," I told him, motioning the guide with a cock of my head to step away from the little crowd and join me a discreet distance away. He picked up on it, and we walked from the gathering unnoticed, eventually sitting on a bench under a tree, well beyond earshot.

"So, as I started to ask, was Mr. . . . . Openshaw lying there all night?"

"Oh, no, no, not at all," answered the guide, whose name was Merle Wills. "In fact, Jack and I left the grounds together last night. But he always got here early every morning, earlier than he had to, really. He was the nervous type, wanting to make sure everything was just so. He said he was just the same way when he worked for the railroad."

"The Rio Grande?"

"Yes. He was a brakeman, retired about three years ago now. He was really excited when he got the chance to come here to work at the fair."

"So, did you work for the railroad as well, Mr. Wills?"

He nodded. "As a station agent in a bunch of small Colorado towns. Places you've likely never heard of like Canon City and Buena Vista and Malta and Dotsero, some of 'em not much more than wide spots in the road. Like Jack, I retired a few years back, and the railroad gave me a chance to come here and work for the summer. They even paid my way in from Colorado on the Denver Zephyr and they're paying my way back after the fair's done, as well. I call that a darned good deal."

"Were you at the fair in '48, too?"

"Oh, no, this tunnel is a brand new thing this season," Wills replied. "Jack was here a year ago, though, also running a projector for movies about the railroad and Colorado."

"I gather that you knew him pretty well."

"Not really. Oh, I did know who he was when we both were with the Rio, of course; the railroad's really a small community when you come right down to it. In truth, I've had a lot more contact with him in this short time at the fair than in all those working years put together."

"Had he ever mentioned anything to you about his health?"

Wills chewed on his lower lip and shook his head. "No sir,

not to me, he didn't. He seemed like he was in pretty good shape for his age."

"And you say that he always was the first one here?"

"Yeah, said he liked to get an early start. On his way here from the rooming house where he was staying, he would always get coffee and a newspaper and sit in the little theater for close to an hour, all by himself. He said it helped loosen him up and get him ready for the day."

"Do you know whether he had a family?"

"Got divorced years ago now. Come to think of it, I don't even know if he ever had any kids. He never mentioned any. If I was to guess, I'd say no." Wills narrowed his eyes at me. "Seems like you're asking an awful lot of questions about a man who just keeled over and died, natural-like. This isn't like those other two men who . . . is it?"

"I honestly don't know that, Mr. Wills. But I will be very interested in what the medical people find out," I said, leaving him and heading back to my typewriter to file a few paragraphs for the two-star edition in my never-ending efforts to keep the *Tribune's* almighty city desk happy.

CHAPTER TWENTY

The poison was easy to buy, Papa, and the rest was easy, too. I had been quietly watching the man who ran the movie projector at the end of that ridiculous phony Rio Grande tunnel. Early every morning, long before the fair opened, he would get to the room where they show the films with a cup of coffee and his newspaper. He would finish about half of his coffee and then he would walk over to the men's toilet a few dozen yards away and be there for ten minutes. He kept a very rigid schedule.

While he was in the toilet today, I went into the empty projection room and put the stuff in his coffee cup. I was gone before he got back. As I now know, he drank from the cup, quickly felt the poison's effects, and tried to walk out of the tunnel. He never made it to the entrance, Papa.

CHAPTER TWENTY-ONE

It did not take long for me to learn the circumstances of Mr. John "Jack" Openshaw's fate. The next morning, I had not been at my desk at the fair for more than ten minutes when my telephone jangled. It was Packy Farmer of the *Herald-American*, calling from Police Headquarters.

"Holy Moses, Snap, you got yourself a regular first-class blood bath out at that fair of yours. How is it that you always find a way to be where the action is?"

"It must be my magnetic personality, Packy. Nice to hear from you. What do you know this morning that I don't?"

"We just got word from Fahey's office, via your replacement Westcott, that the stiff they found lying in that tunnel yesterday morning died of cyanide poisoning."

"Cyanide? No shit?"

"No shit. Apparently the stuff was in his coffee, a healthy dose of it. There was still some java left in the cup, and it was laced to the gills, to say nothing of the poor bastard's stomach."

"It's nice of you to fill me in, Packy. I appreciate it."

"For old times' sake. I'm calling from a pay phone down in the lobby. I didn't want your buddy Westcott to hear me. He's a real pain in the keester, and maybe you can do something with this information."

"I'm touched, but I also know that you, Dirk, and Masters have an ulterior motive."

"What would that be?"

"To see me back there and in league with the three of you. I make your lives easier because I actually do some work. I get the strong impression that Ken Westcott is not exactly a human dynamo."

"Right you are, in spades. Anyway, as I said, I thought you'd like to have the dope. 'Course your guy'll get his byline on this tomorrow morning, but maybe you can find a way to stay on top of the story."

"Packy, if I didn't know you better, I'd think you were trying to foment dissent between two reporters on a competing paper."

"Aw, the *Trib's* not really our competitor, Snap, the *Daily News* is. Your real competition is Dirk O'Farrell and the *Sun-Times*. You go head-to-head in the mornings."

"Okay, although I'd have to call that splitting hairs. Let's face it, as I've said, what you—along with O'Farrell and Masters—*really* want is to have me back there delivering the goods from Fahey every day, and promptly.

"If I were to guess, I'd wager that our Mr. Westcott takes his good old time in meandering downstairs to see the chief every morning. When he finally does bring back news from the Detective Bureau, it's too late for your early editions and for Anson's, too. How am I doing so far?"

I could hear Farmer trying to stifle a chuckle. "All right, let's say that you have got a point. But Snap, you're much better company than Westcott. You gotta admit, the four of us have always hit it off very doggone well. We make a good team, friendly rivals, you might call us."

"Packy, it if were up to me, I never would have left 11th and State. But for whatever reasons, the *Trib* higher-ups thought they had a better idea."

"The way I see it, nothing's ever written in stone," Farmer said. "The more scoops you get out at that fair, the better your chances of getting back here where you belong."

"From your lips to God's ears, Packy."

"Just between us, Snap, d'ya still talk to Fahey at all?"

"Well, we have been known to chew the fat from time to time."

"Ah—I thought so! The chief is quite a fan of yours."

"That so?"

"Yep. You know that curvy blonde with the Veronica Lake hairstyle who's a secretary in the Vice Detail? The one who always wears sweaters?"

"Huh! She's hard to miss."

"Well, we were having coffee across the street the other day, and she told me she was talking to Fahey's secretary, the little brunette with the big smile, who said that the chief really misses having you there. According to her, he looked forward to your daily visits, found them stimulating."

I made no effort to stifle my own laugh: "You could have fooled me. I think he's always just liked the cigarettes I brought him."

"I'm only reporting what I heard. Seems to me that even on the phone you can get more out of Fergus Fahey than Westcott can by sitting down in his office and talking face-to-face."

"Oh, now I understand, Packy. I pump Fergus on the telephone and then pass everything I learn along to you."

He chuckled. "Is that really so bad? It's no different than when you were working with us in the press room. You got the skinny from the chief and then generously shared it with your colleagues."

"True, Packy, but at least there, I got something in return from all of you on your beats, little as it may have been."

"Come on now, Snap, all of us fed each other good stuff," he said, trying without success to sound hurt. "It's just that you had by far the newsiest beat in the building."

"Okay, Packy, I'll stipulate that we helped each other. Now if you'll excuse me, I've got to dash. You never know what interesting people are wandering around the fair just hoping to be interviewed by an enterprising and charming *Tribune* reporter."

After hanging up, I leaned back in my ancient wooden swivel chair and lit a Lucky Strike, blowing smoke rings ceiling-ward. I took a few puffs, then dialed a number.

"Hello, my dear, is the noble defender of the peace taking calls this fine morning?" I asked Elsie Dugo Cascio.

"You can imagine what his mood is," she said, "and in truth, I'm under orders to tell people that he's not in, but my suspicion is he'll make an exception for you, big guy."

"I'm honored, and—" I stopped because she wasn't on the line any longer.

"Yeah?" the chief of detectives gruffed. "What news are you bringing from that miserable fair to make my life even more difficult than it already is?"

"Fergus, Fergus, remember who you're talking to. The guy who for years faithfully brought you Lucky Strikes. The guy who patiently listened to your troubles and dispensed sage counsel."

"Sage counsel, eh? Is that what I was getting from you? I thought it was mostly guff."

"It's tragic how I am treated now that I'm gone from Headquarters. And here I was calling to inquire as to how things are going for you."

"I think you can pretty much guess how things are going for me," Fahey snapped. "Crappy, in a word."

"Anything that you'd care to share with me, Fergus?"

I waited through a long pause at the other end. "Isn't it enough that I already deal with one *Tribune* reporter every day?" he asked plaintively.

"Normally, I'd agree," I told him. "But look at it this way: I'm out here every single day, not counting weekends, and as I have told you before, I can be of some help to you. You know, one more set of eyes and ears."

"But as I've also told you before, your first loyalty is to your newspaper."

"True enough, although that doesn't mean I can't funnel information to you. I can find out all sorts of things that your men can't. Like it or not, a lot of people are leery of the police, as you well know."

"And in return for your help, you will of course expect me to tell you everything that we know."

"Fergus, in all the years you've known me, have I ever—even once—printed anything that you told me was off the record?"

Another pause. "No."

"Well, just because I'm not in the press room at 11th and State anymore doesn't mean I'm less trustworthy than I was before. The more information I have, the more I can help you."

"All right, I'll bite. Just what is it that you want to know?"

"For starters, how are you doing in finding the rifle-loader who disappeared?"

"I haven't told any of this to your man Westcott, so the press doesn't know a thing about it."

"It will stay that way as far as I'm concerned, Fergus."

"We interviewed the other two rifle-loaders and a couple more of the backstage workers who had talked to this mystery man, 'Sam White,' and we've come up with a sketch of what he looks like. Yesterday, copies went out to all the people manning the ticket booths at the main entrance, as well as the private guards, maintenance men, exhibit guides, and others working at the fair."

"What about the person who originally signed him on here?"

Fahey made a sound somewhere between a growl and a snort. "The people at that fair of yours aren't exactly what you might call thorough in their hiring practices. The bird who we talked to barely remembered White and just had him fill out a basic, bare-bones form."

"But didn't he have to give an address where they could mail his checks?"

"The checks are delivered in person to all the fair workers every Friday, so that phony address up on Clarendon that he gave didn't really matter one way or the other."

"Sorry to hear that. Have you had any luck at all with the sketches?"

"Too soon to tell; as I said, we just distributed them yesterday. We haven't told the press—or even that PR guy at the fair—anything about this because we don't want to spook White. The less he knows about us looking for him, the better."

"What about the poisoning?

"You know by now from reading your own Mr. Westcott's piece in the *Trib* that the man found in the tunnel died from a healthy dose of cyanide in his coffee. We figure he took a few swigs of the java back in that little movie room, then felt the poison's effects and ran, or more likely staggered, out toward the tunnel mouth looking for help. The M.E. says he was probably dead before he hit the ground. As you probably are aware, cyanide's the most fast-acting poison there is."

"Yeah, I'm sure I heard that someplace along the way. Dug up any motive?"

Fahey swore. "No more than with either of the others."

"There sure as hell doesn't seem to be any connection among the three," I said. "It makes for a real challenge."

"You wouldn't be thinking about conducting your own rogue investigation now, would you?"

"You know me, Fergus."

"That's precisely why I asked. If you really want to help us like you claim, the best way is to keep your eyes and ears open to anything that seems funny, and to resist the temptation to play Philo Vance, private shamus."

"Message received, sir."

CHAPTER TWENTY-TWO

My next challenge: to lay my hands on one of those sketches of the man who passed himself off as Sam White. I sauntered over to the box office at the main entrance, where half a dozen young women sat at windows taking money and giving the eager masses their tickets to the fair.

In my second week on the job here, I had cranked out a feature on one of the ticket-sellers, a very attractive and sincere local girl named Charlene Miller, who was earning much-needed money to attend Mundelein College up on the city's North Side. After the piece ran—with her smiling and dimpled photograph—I got her a pile of extra copies of the paper for her family and friends, thereby earning her everlasting gratitude, or so I now hoped.

"Hi Mr. Malek!" she chirped when I popped my head into the room where she and the others were dispensing tickets to people lined up six-deep at the windows. "My parents and grandparents all loved the story!"

"Glad to hear it, Charlene. When you can get away, I would like to talk to you briefly. It won't take long, I promise."

"Sure," she said, consulting her wristwatch. "I'm due to take a break in ten minutes. Can you wait that long?"

"For you, of course I can. I'll be just outside the door."

When she came out, I told her that I had a favor to ask.

"Yes, anything that I can do for you," she said with a grin.

"I understand everybody got sketches yesterday of a man who the police are looking for."

"Oh, we did," she said earnestly. "In fact, a whole pile of them got passed out to us."

"Did they now?" I answered. "Well, then . . . here is my favor. As long as there are extras, I'd like to have one of those sketches. I think I may have an idea where this man is."

Her blue eyes widened. "Really?"

I nodded. "But please don't say anything about it to anyone."

"Oh, I won't, Mr. Malek. You know, the man from the police who came in with the pictures asked us not to mention that we had them and were to be on the lookout for this person. But I thought that it was all right to tell you."

"It is, Charlene. Do you think you would be able to go in and get the sketch now? Without letting anyone see you?"

She nodded. "That's easy. There's one in the drawer of my counter that I can slide into my purse. I'll be right back."

She came out a minute later and sidled up to me conspiratorially. "Here it is," she whispered, slipping it out of her purse and pressing it to my chest. "Some day, I would love to know all about this."

"Some day I'm sure that you will," I promised.

"And Mr. Malek?"

"Yes?"

"Thank you again for that article and all the extra copies. I know it made the other girls here a little jealous, but it made everyone in my family so proud of me."

"They should be proud of you," I told her, folding the sheet and putting it in my breast pocket.

Back in the deserted press room, I spread the paper out on my desk, smoothing it. There were two sketches on the page, one head-on, the other a profile. The face looked to be that of a man in his mid-to-late-forties, long and narrow, with prominent cheekbones and a cleft chin. The right profile showed a small mole on his cheek, as Fahey had mentioned to me earlier.

His hair was worn in a flat-top cut, and although the sketches were in black-and-white, the artist had been able to indicate touches of gray at the temples and in the sideburns. His thin mustache also had hints of gray. All in all, the man who called himself Samuel White was an ordinary-looking specimen, not likely to stand out in a crowd.

I refolded the paper, returned it to my breast pocket, and dialed the South Side number of Mr. Pickles Podgorny.

"Damn, Snap, I keep telling you not to call me this early in the day," he groaned.

"But if I try you later, chances are you'll be out wandering around this great metropolis of ours and finding myriad ways to get into trouble."

"I won't dignify that comment with a response. I will tell you, however, that when you wake me earlier than is my normal time of arising, it throws off my timing, and my performance with the pasteboards suffers immeasurably."

"Nonsense, Pickles! I'm convinced you could play for three days nonstop and without sleep and walk away from the table with considerably more greenbacks in your pocket than when you started. So don't give me that crap about needing your beauty sleep. It doesn't wash."

"Spoken like a man who has absolutely no consideration of others and their needs," Pickles groaned.

"If we can steer the discussion away from your needs for a moment, have you found anything out about the identity of our Mr. White?"

That elicited a snort. "What d'you expect, with the flimsy scrap of information you gave me?"

"One can always hope. Tell you what, to at least partially atone for rousting you out of bed at such an ungodly hour, I'll pop for lunch."

"Okay, but this time, I'm not coming all the way over to your overblown fair. Now it's your turn to do some traveling. I'll meet you at 1 o'clock at Jasper's, 30th and Indiana. Best damn ribs in town. A cab'll get you there inside of ten minutes."

For the first and only time, Pickles got to a restaurant before I did. When I walked into the noisy little rib house at 5 after 1, he was settled into a booth with a beer.

"Hope you don't mind I started without you, headline hunter," he said, saluting me with his frosty stein.

"Are you sure that beer won't impair your judgment when you sit down at a game of five-card stud in some secret and shadowy room this evening?"

"Not a chance," he said, licking his lips. "Ah, here's my old friend Millie—that's short for Millicent, by the way. Let's get our orders in before they run out of food."

We gave Millie our requests and I took a sip from the cup of very good coffee she had set before me. "Here's a sketch the police made of our man," I told Pickles, handing the sheet to him.

"Huh! This is about as helpful as your earlier description, Mr. *Tribune*."

"How so?"

"Oh, for God's sake, there's twenty ways from Sunday that this character can change the way he looks and keep walking into the fair, if that's what you think is happening."

"Oh?"

"Sure. He can get rid of that cute little mustache, start wearing glasses that have windowpane lenses, dye his hair black or shave it off and become a baldy, cover his little mole with makeup, get rid of his mustache, stuff his cheeks with cotton, and on and on."

"You sound like an expert on disguises."

"I knew a grifter called 'Faces' Gondorf once. He ran a lot of short-con games around town and seemed to be always one step ahead of the gendarmes. To stay that way, he could change the way he looked to the point where his own mother wouldn't be able to recognize him. He used some sort of clay-like stuff and could give himself a longer nose or ears that stuck out or fatter cheeks, and it looked totally natural. I never saw anything like it. In fact, he said that one time his aunt, who had helped raise him, passed him on 63rd Street in Englewood and had no idea she'd just brushed shoulders with her nephew."

"So whatever happened to this 'Faces' character?"

Pickles shook his head. "Sad story, sad, sad story. He got caught in bed with another man's wife. The husband didn't give two hoots who Faces was or what he looked like; he just shot him dead on the spot, right there in the bedroom. Got him through the pump with a single bullet. So the world lost a truly great artist. Faces could have even given lessons to Lon Chaney, that old-time actor they called 'The Man of A Thousand Faces.'"

"Sad story, indeed," I said as our plates of ribs arrived, along with a bowl full of chubby kosher dills. It was clear that my dining companion was highly esteemed here in Jasper's.

"So, Pickles, to sum things up, you think there's no way we will be able to finger this bird?"

"I didn't say that, but it ain't gonna be easy," he answered between bites of the superb ribs. "I got a few people on it, people who owe me favors."

"I won't ask what those favors are."

"That makes us even, because I won't tell you. You pretty sure our man is behind all three deaths out there on the lakefront?"

"Seems likely to me, although I'll be darned if I can figure out a motive. The three dead men don't seem in any way to be connected, and the shooting is particularly puzzling. How could our man know who was going to get shot, or even *if* anybody would get shot? Most of those actors aren't used to using a rifle, and some of them seemed like they were just pointing their barrels more or less skyward. Was it pure chance that the kid with the live round in his weapon just happened to have been a hunter and knew how to aim?"

He shrugged. "Beats me."

"So here we are, with a shooting, a strangling, a poisoning, and a man with a bogus name and a bogus address. Oh, and also, for the record, a bogus Social Security Number."

"Aren't you glad you're not one of the cops?" Pickles asked, biting into a kosher dill.

"Yeah, although I have to feel for Fahey and his crew. The heat's really on them. But back to basics: I'm curious as to whether you think you can find the mystery man."

"Like I said, you haven't given me much to go on. I've got some friends poking around, but so far, nothing."

"Pickles, level with me. Do you have *anything* at all to go on?"

He finished his ribs and swiped a napkin across his mouth.

"Maybe. For starters, chances are this guy lives up north, probably in Uptown or Edgewater or Rogers Park. He put down an address on Clarendon, which isn't that long or important a street—a northern extension of Halsted, actually—and folks in other parts of town would likely never have heard of it. Also, most people who use a phony moniker keep their same first name because they react naturally when somebody calls to them."

"Interesting. I'm fascinated by the way your mind works, Pickles. So, do you figure the police will think the same way?"

"Maybe, but probably not. But I got something else for you to chew on?"

"Yeah?"

"Why are you so all-fired sure that kid from Iowa who fired the fatal shot is clean?"

"What makes you question it?"

"I been thinking some since our last lunch. This shooter is a would-be actor, right?"

"Right, he's been in a few plays, small local stuff."

"And the guy he shot?"

"Also what you'd call an aspiring actor."

"In the same kinds of theaters?"

"I suppose, little troupes in storefronts, lucky to get two dozen customers."

"Don't you find that interesting?"

"Look, Pickles, a majority of the cast members in that pageant probably have done some acting at one level or another."

He sipped coffee and made a face. "Okay, but still, doesn't it strike you as more than a coincidence that somehow, the only one who had firearms experience *just happens* to get the only weapon that has a live round, and he *just happens* to shoot, and kill, another actor who's about his same age?"

"Your point being?"

"One, maybe our lad from Muscatine loaded the live round himself. Two, maybe, just maybe, he and the poor sap who's now pushing up posies were competing for the same role or roles in some plays being cast around town."

"That's preposterous!"

"Why?"

"I met the shooter, Pickles. He was terribly shaken."

"For Christ's sake, mister hard-bitten reporter who sometimes acts like a babe-in-the-woods, he's an *actor*. Please don't tell me that he fooled you."

"Pickles, even if these two were in competition for parts in local plays, that's hardly motive enough for murder. Most of the roles they'd be likely to get at this stage of their careers would barely pay the rent."

"Actors are a strange lot, some of them downright looney. Hell, I knew of a guy years back named Mahaffey, I think it was. I only ran into him two or three times, but that was enough to mark him as real screwy—"

"Hold on now, that's hardly a scientific study."

"I'm not done yet," Pickles said, holding up a palm. "This puffed-up ham was in some sort of neighborhood theater production out along Archer Avenue on the Southwest Side of the city, real amateur stuff. A reviewer for the local weekly paper in that area panned his acting, and the self-styled thespian threw a fit. He barged into the newspaper office where the reviewer worked and brandished a sword that had been used in the play, 'Hamlet' I think it was. He swung it at the poor bastard, who was sitting at his typewriter, and damned near cut off his ear before some others in the office wrestled the sword away from him."

"I have a vague memory of reading about that at the time," I chuckled.

"It was no laughing matter," Pickles snapped. "He tried to

kill the reporter, plain and simple. You of all people should sit up and take notice of that. But my point here is that actors are a high-strung and unpredictable bunch."

"Okay, even assuming the boy from Muscatine might—and I say might—have planned the shooting, how do you explain the other two deaths? Why would the kid have killed them, if he was even still in town?"

"I dunno. I'm just pointing out that you've always got to look at a lot of different angles."

"I appreciate that thought, and I'll try to find out if these two actors were indeed in competition for a role. But I think that we should concentrate on our 'Mr. White,'"

Pickles nodded grimly. "All right," he said, but there wasn't much conviction behind it.

"What's the next step?"

"He scowled. For the pittance you've given me, I should give away all my secrets to you?"

"Not necessarily. But let's see if I can think like you do. You—or somebody you know—walks into various bars in Uptown and Edgewater and asks if 'Sam' has been around. How am I doing?"

"Fair, although part of the secret is knowing just which saloons among the many up that way are the most likely spots to find our man. That's where some of my acquaintances can be helpful."

"And if you do find him?"

"We'll play that by ear, and very, very carefully," Pickles said. "And I know that you, being an honorable man, will make it worth our while."

I smiled but said nothing, wondering just how much cash my bosses would let me dole out to informants in quest of a scoop.

CHAPTER TWENTY-THREE

Days went by with no word from Pickles, but I was hardly surprised. I had given him a near-impossible task, one that was not likely to smoke out one "Samuel White." On a positive note, days also went by without another violent death on the fairgrounds.

I continued to dig up feature stories at the fair, with more than a little help from Fred Metzger and his eager-to-please intern, Rob Taylor. The two of them kept the master schedule of visiting dignitaries and gave me first crack at these so-called luminaries before alerting other newspapers, first the Chicago dailies, then papers in nearby cities like Milwaukee, Springfield, Rockford, Gary, and Aurora.

The folks I did stories on included a U.S. senator from Kansas (blowhard), a way-over-the-hill Hollywood leading man whose principal claim to fame was seven marriages (egomaniac), a family of Austrian acrobats who performed in the Special Events Arena on the lakefront (difficult to communicate with), and a fifty-seven-year-old farmer (aw-shucks homespun variety) who had ridden a bicycle to the fair all the way from his home town of Klamath Falls, Oregon, "because I love trains. After all this darn pedaling, I'm going to ride one all the way back home. As for my bicycle, it can ride in the baggage car while I eat steaks and drink good wine in the diner."

At about the time that I had gotten my fill of grinding out pieces that had all the substance of cotton candy, a legitimate personality loomed on the fair's horizon.

"It is official!" Fred Metzger boomed as he toddled into the press room one Monday morning, followed by Rob. "Walt Disney himself is en route to Chicago on the Super Chief from California and will be arriving here tomorrow afternoon. According to the schedule we received from his studio, he will be at the fair all day Wednesday, and maybe Thursday, as well. He is traveling with one of his movie animators, a fellow named Kimball, who I understand to be famous in his own right."

"I seem to recall that way back when I first arrived here, you promised me the first opportunity to interview the legendary Mr. Disney," I told Metzger.

"Yes I did, and that still holds," he bubbled. "After all, you are the only full-time reporter here, and you are most definitely entitled to that. I thought maybe we could set up a lunch for you and Mr. Disney, and perhaps his sidekick as well. I would suggest the Chessie Club, which is the best restaurant on the grounds. But please don't quote me on that—I can't show even the least little bit of favoritism, and of course there are a lot of excellent eating places at the fair."

"Of course there are. Don't worry, my lips are sealed."

"Good, good. I'll be happy to make a reservation for Wednesday. Is that okay with you?"

"Hey, if it's okay with the one and only Walt Disney, then I'd have to say that it's certainly okay with me as well," I told him.

At noon on Wednesday, I sat at a table for four in the elegant dining car operated by the Chesapeake & Ohio Railroad and named for "Chessie," a cat used in the line's advertising. I had been there about five minutes when the white-jacketed steward brought two men over to me.

"Hi, I'm Walt Disney," said a smiling, dark-haired specimen in his forties who might have passed for an aging matinee idol, with his slicked back dark hair, thin mustache, and chiseled profile. We shook hands as he gestured to his companion.

"This, Mr. Malek, is the great Ward Kimball, beyond question the finest, most creative animator in our business. Without Ward, there would have been no 'Pinocchio,' no 'Dumbo' or 'Snow White and the Seven Dwarfs,' or . . . well, I believe that you get the idea. The man is an unquestioned genius, the likes of which the motion picture world will never again see."

Kimball, a full-faced fellow with what I later learned was a perpetual grin, reddened slightly at the praise from his boss but made no effort to contradict him.

"Please sit down, both of you," I said. "This is, so I have been told, the best dining spot at the fair, although I have not tried it yet."

"Seems nice to me," Disney said, nodding and looking around. "So, Mr. Malek, I understand you are a reporter with the *Chicago Tribune*."

"Guilty as charged," I replied as a waiter took our cocktail orders.

"Well, I grew up on the *Tribune*," he said. "As you may know, I spent a lot of time in Chicago in my early years."

"He sure did," Kimball chimed in. "After we left the fair last night, I wanted to visit some of your great jazz clubs, but Walt here insisted on showing me the Elevated lines he rode way back when, including the station near his home where he boarded the trains."

Disney chuckled. "Yes, I'm afraid I took him away from his beloved jazz. But for all of Ward's complaining, he really didn't mind all that much. He's a railroad buff, like me."

"On that subject, how are both of you enjoying the fair?"

Disney started to reply but Kimball waved him off. "Let me tell you, Walt has been in hog heaven ever since we got here. They even let him drive one of the oldest locomotives in the pageant this morning. They dressed him up in a frock coat and a top hat and away he went. He looked like he fit right in!"

"Ward's been having just as much fun as me, and they dressed him up in period clothes, too," Disney said as I scribbled some notes. "He loves trains so much that he's got an outdoor railroad running all around his property back home in California, and it has inspired me to build one, too, as soon as I can talk my wife into the idea."

"So of course with your interest in railroading, you came into town on the train, right?" I asked.

"Did we ever!" Kimball enthused. "In adjoining drawing rooms on the Super Chief, no less. Talk about luxury; those Santa Fe folks really gave us the royal treatment. We even got to ride up front in the engine for awhile and Walt pulled on the whistle cord several times going across the desert. When we got back to our car, he just sat staring off into space. I've never seen him look so happy."

Our drinks arrived, and both Disney and I lit cigarettes, he a Philip Morris and me a Lucky Strike. Kimball shot a disapproving look at his boss, then at me, but he said nothing.

During drinks and our meal, Disney peppered me with questions about Chicago—its politics, its sports teams, and even the Dearborn Street subway, currently under construction. I gave him my thoughts, for what they were worth.

"Do you feel that the city is getting rid of its reputation as a crime capital?" he asked.

"Maybe to a degree," I said, "although the Syndicate's still a force, no question."

He looked thoughtful. "We understand there's been some bad trouble right here on the grounds."

"Yes, three deaths." I proceeded to tell them about the circumstances and details of all three. "I can't see any connection among them whatever," I said as Disney torched another Philip Morris. "There's no evidence the same person was involved in each of them. It's a puzzler."

The filmmaker pursed his lips as if in deep thought, remaining silent for half a minute. "If I were to hazard a guess," he finally said, "it would be that one individual is somehow behind all of this mischief. And that individual has a grudge—clearly a most intense one—against railroads."

"You mean railroads in general?" I asked.

"I'm not about to trust my guess that far," Disney said, "but it's certainly possible. One death at the Rio Grande exhibit, another at the Illinois Central area, and the shooting at that pageant, where all sorts of railroads are represented."

"Well, one thing is certain," I said. "The people running this show are jumpier than a circus clown on a pogo stick, and with good reason. But that's enough of this grim news. I'm supposed to be doing a feature on you for the paper. I think it's fair to say that you're enjoying your visit, right?"

"Immensely!" Disney boomed, causing people at nearby tables to turn and look our way. "As Ward told you, these fine folks have pretty much given us the run of the place. I was delighted when they let me drive that one engine—the DeWitt Clinton, it's called. Dates way back to the 1830s, I was told. And this is the original train from those days, not a replica like some of the others in the pageant. I was surprised at just how easy it was to operate."

"What he's really saying," Kimball put in with a wink, "is that he didn't derail the darn thing."

"After your visit here, will you be heading back to Hollywood?" I asked.

"Not right away. We're going to swing by Henry Ford's Greenfield Village over in Michigan. I've got an idea, Mr. Malek, for a sort of amusement park, something that's never been done before."

"Don't get him started on this," Ward Kimball said with a laugh.

"No, please, go on," I insisted.

Disney got a dreamy look in his eyes. "These last two days have really helped me decide what I'd like to do. I want to build a new type of park for . . . well, for kids. Although something that adults will enjoy, too. Seeing all these different 'villages' at the fair—a New Orleans neighborhood, an Indian pueblo, a Florida setting, a Wild West town—has really spurred me to get started on this. And maybe I can get some more ideas at Greenfield Village."

"Sounds pretty ambitious," I observed.

"Ambitious, yes it is," he said, nodding. "But it could be great fun, too. Like here, there would be trains. I could see us having one like the old-time western Gold Gulch Central Railroad you've got. I'd also like to have a Main Street with an open-air trolley car. I can picture train rides of one kind and another all over the place in my new park."

"I warned you not to get him wound up," Kimball said, grinning and wagging an index finger at me. "All the way here on the Super Chief, he talked about a park, and I'm sure that he'll also be talking about it all the way back to the West Coast, as well. But that's okay; I'm a good listener. Also, he *is* my boss."

After lunch, Phil Muller met us outside the Chessie Club dining car and took some photos of Disney and Kimball. I shook hands with both of them and went back to the press room to crank out my feature story on their visit.

I touched on Walt Disney's Chicago roots, then concentrated on his and Kimball's love of trains and their activities at the fair, particularly Disney's turn at driving locomotives across the stage in the pageant.

I did not, however, write about his idea for an amusement park. It was clearly a wacky pipe dream floating around in the hyperactive mind of a man who should stick to making animated films.

CHAPTER TWENTY-FOUR

I probably was every bit as relieved as the fair's officials when Disney left Chicago for his visit to Henry Ford's famous museum over in Michigan. At least he wouldn't be the target of some madman. At dinner, I filled Catherine in on my meeting with the celebrity from Hollywood.

"So what was he like?" she asked.

"A decent guy, laughs a lot, seems to really enjoy life."

"Is he young, old? I've never even seen a photograph of the man, as famous as he is."

I gave her my assessment, including the part about him resembling what I thought of as a motion picture leading man slightly past his prime.

"I wonder if he was at all worried about coming here, given all that's happened at the fair lately," she mused.

"If so, he certainly didn't show it. He just seemed so happy to be there. Both he and Kimball are absolutely batty about anything to do with trains. They were like two little kids who got turned loose in a candy store."

"Nice to have a hobby like that."

"I suppose. We did talk briefly about the murders. He thinks they were done by somebody with a long-standing grudge against railroads."

"What does your Mr. Fahey think?"

"We really haven't talked much about a motive. In fact, with me out at the fair, we don't talk all that much at all."

"I'll bet he misses your daily meetings."

"I think what he really misses more than anything else is the free Lucky Strikes I doled out to him for years. My replacement doesn't smoke and wouldn't deign to feed someone else's habit. But you know, I really do believe Fergus sometimes uses me as a sounding board."

"It also could be that he trusts your judgment," she said as she began to clear the table.

"Maybe. Or maybe he just gets lonesome shut away in that office most of the day with piles of paperwork and is glad for a little company, even if that company comes in the form of a wiseacre."

"I think that you should tell him what Walt Disney said."

"You mean about a grudge against railroads in general possibly being a motive?"

"Why not?"

"You're right, why not, although it may already have occurred to him. I'll do it tomorrow. How 'bout you wash the dishes and I'll dry?"

"I like that offer very much."

CHAPTER TWENTY-FIVE

The next morning, I dropped into my desk chair in the fair's press room and immediately dialed Fergus Fahey's office. "Is he in his chambers this fine summer morning?" I asked Elsie.

"He is indeed, and in none too good a mood, I might add," she said.

"Why should this day be different than any other? Think he'll talk to me?"

"I'd be surprised if he didn't, but we won't know until we try. Hold on."

"Geez, you call so often that it's like you're still working here," the chief grumped when he came on the line.

"To think I felt that you'd be just tickled to hear from me, Fergus. You know how I like to stay in touch with old friends."

"Is that right? Well, it's not hard to figure out why you're really calling. I'm afraid I don't have any news for you."

"Ditto at this end. But I do have a couple of thoughts, if you're interested."

"I'm willing to listen to them, if only to show you just how bad off things are around here."

"I'll ignore that remark and plunge ahead. First, has anybody checked to see whether the actor who fired the shot and the actor who died were in competition for a role at some local theater?"

Fahey made a growling sound. "You're suggesting that somebody would kill over a part in a play? Snap, you've been reading too many detective magazines. Come back into the real world. Besides, how would that account for the other two deaths?"

"Okay, I'll admit it seemed like a long shot, but any port in a storm, as they say. Next, what about the theory that the killer is somebody who has a grudge against some railroad, or maybe against *all* railroads?"

"Now whose theory would that be?" the chief demanded.

"Nobody's in particular, but what do you think about it?"

After a long pause, Fahey swore and admitted that, "I've played around with that theory, too, and I suppose it's as good as anything else I've heard, although how in God's name you'd ever locate somebody with a grudge like that is beyond my simple mind. That last is off the record."

"Of course it is. Your mind is a lot of things, but simple is not one of them. All right, I just wanted you to know that I'm trying to help."

"So noted. Now if you'll excuse me, I have a commissioner to meet with."

My next call was to Hazel, the longest-serving staffer in the *Tribune* reference room, or morgue, as it is widely known in our business. Each Christmastime, I give her a bottle of her favorite single-malt Scotch, an investment that has paid off many times over. And its cost is not hidden somewhere in my expense account, but comes directly out of my own battered billfold.

"Good morning, oh noble guardian of the archives," I said when she answered. "I trust your day is going well."

"I haven't been here long enough this morning for things to be really screwed up yet, Snap. What can I do for you?"

"I'm so glad you asked. I'm looking for somebody who doesn't like railroads."

"Doesn't like—oh, that's right, you're out at the Railroad Fair this summer, aren't you? I suppose this has something to do with all those croakings you've had, huh?"

"I've always liked your use of the vernacular, Hazel, m'dear. It's so . . . so *you*."

"Aw shucks, Snap, I'm just a simple country girl who got lured to the glamour of the big city from the farmlands of the great state of Nebraska. You can take the girl out of the boondocks, but you can't . . . Well, you know the rest of the saying."

"Right. Anyway, here's what I'm looking for: Railroad accidents, wrecks, mishaps where there were deaths and/or controversy."

"Just how far back would you like me to go, Laddie?"

"Oh, say twenty years or so."

"Also, are we confining ourselves to the Chicago area?"

"Not necessarily, but I think that's where I'll find what I'm looking for—if it's even there at all."

"I suppose you need the stuff sometime yesterday?" she sighed.

"Well, let's just say the sooner the better." I gave her my phone number at the fair.

"Only for you would I do this. I assume you're going to swing by the Tower after I get stuff pulled together."

"As usual, you assume correctly, Hazel. Have I told you lately what a gem you are?"

"Can all that sweet talk, buster. I'm on the case for you, although heaven knows, it may take awhile. I do have a few other duties around here from time to time, you know."

"Ah, but you love these special assignments. They add spice to your day."

"Your definition of 'spice' is interesting, Snap. Sometime, you ought to spend a few hours here diving into file drawers, poring through grubby envelopes, and pulling out yellowed clippings that look like they're about to come apart in your hands. It's really exciting, yes sir, it is."

"Now Hazel, there's no call for you to get sarcastic. Consider that you may very well be furthering the cause of justice."

"I'll hold that thought close to my heart in the hours that lie ahead. Sorry to cut this delightful conversation short, but I have those other duties I mentioned, strange as that may seem to you."

I excused her with profound thanks and prepared for my next interview, which was with the man who operated the thirty-five-foot Paul Bunyan robot at the Chicago & North Western Railway exhibit.

The robot moved, shook hands, and talked about its exploits as a fabled lumberjack in the great northern forests of Wisconsin, Minnesota, and Upper Michigan, regions where the railroad operated. The fair's run was not yet half over, and it was clear that I was running out of story ideas.

CHAPTER TWENTY-SIX

I have been spending time lately walking along the shore, Papa. So much of the fair runs right down to the water's edge, and in the case of the Cypress Gardens Thrill Show, Lake Michigan itself gets to have a starring role. It is now the moment for the grand old lake to play a bigger part in our own plans, too, yours and mine. The next time you hear from me, you will understand what I mean and I know that you will applaud my actions . . .

CHAPTER TWENTY-SEVEN

To my pleasant surprise, the man who was the voice of Paul Bunyan turned out to be an entertaining interview. The old fellow, named Nils Ericsson, had himself been a lumberjack, sawing away in the forests of Northern Wisconsin and Minnesota beginning in the early years of the century.

Ericsson, who looked like he could still swing a mean axe, was a born storyteller, and despite being "in the neighborhood of the upper seventies"—he resolutely declined to give his exact age—had a strong, clear voice with a slight Scandinavian tinge, an asset for one acting as Bunyan's alter-ego and describing the fictional giant's adventures to fairgoers.

"My daddy was a lumberjack too," he declared as we talked at a picnic table under a tree near the Bunyan exhibit. "He died at ninety-four, still as strong as a bear, but he almost didn't live to see thirty-five."

"Hmm. Something to do with a falling tree, I suppose?"

"No, no!" he rumbled, waving my question away with a meaty and calloused hand. "He was too smart for anything like that to happen. It was back in the fall of '71, same year as that big fire that you had down here. Well, Wisconsin had some powerful strong fires its own at the very same time. The worst one was in a little place called Peshtigo, horrible it was. Said to be the deadliest fire in American history. It was reported that as many as 2,500 may have died, nobody ever knew for sure. Lots of them got buried in mass graves.

"Anyway, my Daddy happened to be in that very neck of the woods at the time, working for a big lumber outfit out of Appleton, I think I heard him tell. They were doing some cutting up north of Peshtigo, near the little burg of Menominee, Michigan. Well, at first it seemed as they were at a safe distance from the fire, but then the wind shifted and the flames moved north fast, and I do mean fast. Daddy and his crew of three or four had all they could do to get themselves on foot over to the shore of Green Bay about the time it was starting to get dark.

"A fishing boat was about a quarter-mile off shore. My Daddy said the fishermen on board were watching the flames. He and his men hollered and waved their arms and jumped up and down until the boat finally came in and picked them up. Not a moment too soon, you might say. Them flames eventually went right up to the shore, and it was said that the water in Green Bay got downright uncomfortable."

"A close call."

"Yessir, very close. They was among the lucky ones."

Ericsson spun more tales—about his life as a lumberjack, a general store owner, a semi-professional wrestler, and the operator of a small carnival that moved from town to town around the Upper Midwest.

"Them carnies can be a mean darn bunch sometimes," he said, "but they never messed with me, I can tell you. I made sure they knew about my wrestling days as 'Sven, the Savage Swede.' I had a beard back then, and I dyed it yellow, along with my hair."

"You must have been quite a sight."

"Or quite a fright," he said, roaring at his own cleverness.

Now that Ericsson had been wound like an alarm clock, he kept on going, regaling me with tales of his wrestling adventures and the bizarre cast of characters he had to ride herd on while running his ragtag carnival. I finally told him I had plenty of material, plus a deadline that was coming up fast. I had asked for a photographer, and sure enough, it turned out to be none other than Phil Muller, who made some shots of Ericsson grinning, hands on hips, with the Paul Bunyan robot looming behind him and wearing a grin of its own.

"Somehow you look different today," I told Muller.

He grinned. "Took you awhile to notice. Shaved off my mustache. The wife got tired of it, said it made me look like an old-time movie villain."

"I think she had a point. It seems like you're around almost every day now," I told Muller after Ericsson had gone back to spinning yarns at the North Western exhibit.

"Snap old pal, I saw what a damned sweet deal you have out here, so I decided to hitch my wagon to your star. Besides, I grew up around trains; I come from a railroad family."

"I guess I never knew that."

"Yep, my late father was a brakeman, worked on both the B&O and the Milwaukee Road."

"My late father was involved in trains, too, in a sense. He was a Chicago streetcar motorman for probably close to forty years."

"Hope he got treated better by his bosses than my old man did," Phil said quietly, packing up his gear. "Keep finding good feature subjects here, Snap, and I'll find ways to wangle the assignments. We make a good team, you know. A damned good team."

CHAPTER TWENTY-EIGHT

This one was a little harder for me, Papa. First I had to sneak up behind him. I did not want to have to look into his face. As he did each night, he was cleaning up garbage along the shore—fair programs and hot dog wrappers and such, and putting it all into a gunnysack. Fortunately, I think he may have been somewhat hard of hearing, and I was wearing soft-soled shoes. He didn't make more than a slight groan when I hit him with that hammer.

I know that the blow didn't kill him, but he was so dazed that the rest was easy in the darkness. I held his face down in the water. He struggled for a little while, not long at all, and then stopped moving. Like the others, Papa, he was old, and probably would not have lived that much longer anyway . . .

CHAPTER TWENTY-NINE

My feature on Nils Ericsson, a.k.a. Sven, the Savage Swede, ran on Page 5 of the next day's paper, along with a two-column Phil Muller photo of the former lumberjack and wrestler. It was the best play by far that any of my features from the fair had been given. I had gotten so that I took some delight in small victories. But I nevertheless knew that I was still a "feature writer," a pejorative term in the vocabulary of the hard-news reporter.

"Very nice article you had this morning," Fred Metzger said as he stuck his head into the press room. "I just wish that the other papers in town gave us the kind of play that the *Trib* does."

"Well, in fairness to them, we've got more space to fill than anybody else, so I guess it figures," I told him as I looked up from reading the tabloid *Sun-Times*. "Say, Fred, how do you feel about the police presence around here now?"

Metzger shook his head and scowled. "I'm aware that the department has beefed up the plainclothes numbers, but there are still way too many uniformed men around for my taste. It has to make people nervous to see them."

"I don't think most of the visitors even notice. They're too busy having fun. Besides, it's just possible that the extra cops are the reason we haven't had any more incidents."

"Could be," he said without conviction. Just then, the phone rang in his office, and he dashed off to answer it as I tried to figure out where my next feature was coming from.

My thought processes, such as they were, got interrupted by Metzger's keening, which cut through the thin partition like a butcher knife. "What! Oh no, oh no, no, no," he yelled.

I ran next door and saw him slumped in his desk chair, head in hand and receiver pressed to his ear. "Where? Oh Christ! Have they been called? Yes, Yes. Phone the fair manager's office. They'll want to cancel the morning show if they haven't already."

He hung up and stared down at his desk blotter, head in hands. "What is it, Mr. Metzger?" asked his summer intern, Rob, who had come over from his small desk in the corner.

"Another one," Metzger muttered, "another one, another one."

"Where?" I demanded.

"In . . . the water, the lake."

"Where, Goddammit? Where, Fred?" I grabbed the hunched-over PR man by the shoulders and shook him until I thought his teeth would rattle.

"Cypress Gardens," he said, putting his head down on his desk.

"Have the police been notified?"

He raised his head long enough to nod. I tore out of the building, vaguely aware that Rob followed in my wake, and I jogged northeast toward the shoreline area where the Cypress Gardens Thrill Show was held, and where a few weeks earlier I had interviewed one of the leggy "Aqua Belles."

The bleachers facing the water were empty, and a sign at the entrance read "Ten A.M. Show Canceled." On the beach, four men, two of them in uniforms, stood over a body.

As I neared the gathering, I heard one of the uniformed men, a fair security guard, tell the others that ". . . and when I came by this morning about the time the fair opened, I saw somethin' floating about fifteen or twenty feet out." He pointed into the calm waters of the lake.

"At first I thought it was maybe a log, we get a few of them floating by, but then I seen that it was . . . Anyhow, I waded out and dragged this poor feller in, what was left of him, that is."

The body on the sand looked to be in his sixties and stocky, with short gray hair. His face was only slightly discolored and not bloated, indicating he hadn't been in the water all that long.

"Any idea who he is?" asked a man in a suit, who turned out to be a tall, lean police detective with a beak-like schnozz named Moritz. I had met him once several years back.

The security guard shook his head. "Nope, although I think I've seen him around here. He might be somebody who worked for the water show, as a sort of janitor, I guess you could say."

"Who are you?" Moritz said, suddenly aware that I had become part of the little gathering.

"Steve Malek, *Tribune* reporter. I'm assigned to the fair full time."

He cast me a dubious clance. "How'd you get over here so fast?"

I explained the sequence of events in the administration building, including the phone call to Fred Metzger. "I assume somebody in fair security had phoned him about this."

"I'm the one who did," the other man wearing a suit put in. "My name is Carl Mason. I am one of the assistant managers of the fair. I came over here as fast as I could, and I just posted the sign canceling the morning show."

Moritz scowled. "Know who this is?" he asked, motioning to the body.

"Yes I do," Mason said with a glum nod. "He's Alec Cunningham, a maintenance man who's assigned to the water show. His job is to clean up the area after the last show every night, then come first thing in the morning and rake this stretch of beach in front of the grandstands where the acts take place. We like it always to be looking neat here, just like the rest of the fairgrounds."

"What else can you tell me about him?" the detective barked at Mason.

"Not a lot. I seem to remember that he's an old-time railroad man who was at the fair last year, too. I believe he retired some years ago from the Chicago & Eastern Illinois, where he worked as a dispatcher or something like that."

"There looks to be a good-sized lump on his head," I said.

"Your input is duly noted," Moritz remarked stiffly, scribbling in a notebook. "This fair is having its problems, isn't it?" he said to Mason, pointedly turning his back on me.

The assistant manager nodded, hands in pockets, staring down at the body of Cunningham. "Anybody have anything further to add?" the detective asked.

We all—Mason, the security guard, Rob Taylor, and I—remained silent. Moritz turned to the uniformed cop with a scowl. "Get a couple more men over here and secure the area. The M.E. should be on his way. All right everybody, class dismissed," he snapped. "And that definitely includes you, Mr. *Tribune* man."

When I got back to the administration building, I popped my head into Metzger's office, but he wasn't around. "Any idea where he might've gone?" I asked Rob, who had walked back with me.

"No, maybe to see the fair manager. He's really shaken."

"With good reason," I said, going back to my phone, where I placed a call to the *Trib*. "Well, it's happened again," I said to Hal Murray on the city desk. "Another stiff at the fair."

"Yeah, we're just getting the word. That place of yours has become a real bloodbath. Okay, what've you got for me?"

I read him my sketchy information, and he transferred me to rewrite so we could at least squeeze a bulletin into the next edition. I contemplated calling Fergus Fahey but vetoed it, at least for the present. He was going to be pulling his hair out by the roots, and he didn't need me asking him questions or even giving him my eyewitness account. He could, and would, get the same information from Detective Moritz, who would no doubt mention somewhere in his report that a pesky *Tribune* reporter promptly happened upon the death scene.

CHAPTER THIRTY

The fourth death at the fair really set the daily papers off like dogs tearing into a slab of raw meat. Every one of them gave the latest killing their banner headline, with the *Herald-American's* WHERE WILL IT ALL END? printed in red ink, an old Hearst device. Reading our piece the next morning, which carried a joint byline—Westcott and me—I learned that the victim, Cunningham, 69, was the father of three and the grandfather of four, lived in the southern suburb of Blue Island, and had probably been dead anywhere from six to ten hours when his body was discovered.

The police confirmed that death was by drowning but a blow to the head with the predictable "blunt instrument" probably first rendered the victim unconscious. He was found in less than two feet of water.

The *Herald-American* carried a front-page editorial in which the paper offered $10,000 for information leading to the arrest of "person or persons responsible for the violent deaths at our fair."

The *Trib* also weighed in on the subject, although in its normal place on the editorial page:

SHUTTER THE FAIR?

It has been suggested in some quarters that because of the ongoing violence at the Chicago Railroad Fair, the exposition should be shut down.

Nonsense.

In a civilized and democratic society, events must under no circumstances be dictated by fear and terror. We have full and abiding confidence that our law-enforcement agencies will hunt down and bring to justice whoever is responsible for the crimes that have been committed along the lakefront.

To those among you who insist the fair must close to protect the masses, we answer that this is precisely the type of action that terrorists seek to accomplish. To yield to such a move is to cede victory to lawlessness and anarchy. We only need to study history to see this scenario played out again and again.

Let the gates stay open.

Fred Metzger, looking haggard and with shoulders sloping more than usual, appeared in the doorway of the press room as I put down my paper. "I just want to tell you that I think the *Tribune's* coverage of . . . of all this . . . is the most measured, and the most responsible," he said.

I nodded my thanks. "By the way, if we can move on to less somber matters, have you got any feature ideas for me? My cupboard is now every bit as bare as poor Old Mother Hubbard's."

"Yes, that's the other thing I stopped by to tell you," he said, pulling a folded sheet from his breast pocket. "Here's something that might be interesting: Three generations of a railroad family from Indiana are coming in today, should be here by ten or so."

"It's a possibility," I said without enthusiasm.

"Well, anyway, I'm giving you the right of first refusal. The *Daily News* has been after me to throw some features their way, but they won't even bother to send someone out here until I've lined something up for them," he sniffed, sounding offended.

"Okay, I'm willing to be persuaded. Tell me about this Indiana bunch."

He consulted the sheet. "Let's see now, the grandson is a conductor on New York Central passenger trains, he's . . . twenty-eight. His father, who's fifty, works as a fireman, also on the NYC, but on freights. And the grandfather, seventy-four, is a retired engineer who worked for more than forty-five years on the Nickel Plate Road. He was at the throttle of some of their crack limiteds."

"Well, why not give it a try?" I said, not having anything else on my assignment sheet at the moment. "Lead me to 'em."

The Indiana railroading family, name of Ferguson, turned out to be dishwater dull, and that included the wives. I couldn't get a single decent anecdote out of the lot. Even good old Grandpa, who'd started in the business just after the turn of the century, had almost nothing to say about how things had changed in the last fifty years.

"More diesels today," was one pithy observation of his. When I asked if that was a good thing, he said, "In some ways yes, in some ways no. At least you don't have none of them doggone cinders with the diesels." Swell, Gramps, thanks for your help.

The younger generations were no better. When I asked the twenty-eight-year-old conductor if he'd like to see his son go into railroading, he thought for a minute and replied, "Well, I guess that'd be up to him, wouldn't it? When he gets older, of course, that is."

The old Indian in the Santa Fe village who I'd conducted the non-interview with on my first day at the fair was looking more exciting all the time. I now wished I had let the folks at the *Daily News* tackle this one.

But I did manage to stitch together a piece, embellishing the bland quotes I got from the three men and their equally taciturn wives. The day's only surprise came when the photog who showed up was not Phil Muller.

"He got sent to a fire out near the Stockyards," said Chuck Mills, who tried manfully but without success to get a smile out of any one of the bunch, including the kids. The group shot of the Hoosier clan that ran in the next day's edition looked like a funeral gathering.

After I had finished the article and dictated it to Williamson on the rewrite desk, I was about to leave the empty press room and grab a ham sandwich at the Cupboard Restaurant near the main gate when my phone rang. It was Pickles Podgorny.

"Lordy be! What're you doing up at this hour, poker puss? It's barely past noon."

"Now what kind of greeting is that for a man who has some information for you? Let's show a little respect," huh?"

"Whoops, sorry. All right, fire away. You have my full attention."

"It appears that we may have located your mystery man."

"The elusive Mr. Sam White?"

"The selfsame."

"Well, go on, go on," I prompted.

"Nothing absolutely definite, you understand, but one of my . . . acquaintances made the rounds of a goodly number of the watering holes in Uptown and Lakeview the last few evenings, asking bartenders if 'Sam' had been in lately."

"And?"

"Don't interrupt, I'm telling the story. Last night, my acquaintance, let's just call him Benny, popped into a little joint on Wilson just west of Broadway, asking his question, and the barkeep said, 'You mean Sam Whitnauer?'"

"Benny said he didn't know the last name, only that this "Sam" owed him some money. Then he described him. The barkeep said that sounded like Whitnauer, all right, and that he usually wandered in around ten or ten-thirty most nights."

"So Benny waited for him?"

"I told you not to interrupt. No, he likes to avoid face-to-face scenes, given some of his past activities and adventures with the law. He left the saloon without even buying a drink and went across the street, where he leaned against a lamppost and waited.

"A few minutes after ten, a guy comes along on foot and shuffles into the bar. Benny, who's seen the sketch you gave me, says no question, that's him. The lighting's pretty good along that stretch of Wilson, and Benny says everything checks out—the flattop haircut, the little mustache, and he also thought he could make out a mole on this Sam's right cheek."

"Nice work, Pickles, very nice work indeed. I believe we may indeed have our man in the person of one Mr. Sam Whitnauer. By the way, as a point of interest, what's the story on your boy Benny?"

"Why?"

"Just curious. I always like to know who I'm relying on."

"So now you don't trust your old pal Pickles?" he sniffed.

"I didn't say that, and you'll notice that I also didn't ask for Benny's real name. Tell me a little about him."

There was silence at the other end for several seconds. "Okay, let's just say that over the years, he's run a lot of two-man short-cons, particularly the old 'fiddle game.'"

"What's that?"

"You mean to say, Mister 'Man of the World,' that you have never heard of the fiddle game?"

"Guess that's what I'm saying."

"You've got a lot to learn about life in the big city, Snap. Okay, here's how it works: Guy Number One goes into a restaurant in shabby clothes and carrying a violin in its case. He eats, then tells the owner he left his wallet at home, which is nearby, and needs to go and get it, but that he'll leave the violin, which he dearly loves, as security. Are you with me?"

"So far."

"Then just after he leaves, presumably to get money, Guy Number Two walks in, notices the fiddle case, and seems interested. He inquires as to what's inside, and the owner says a violin. Guy Number Two asks to see it. When owner shows it to him, Number Two raves about it, saying it's a centuries-old Stradivarius, worth thousands. He offers big bucks to buy it but says that he can't hang around. He leaves his business card with the restaurateur and asks him to give the card to Guy Number One when he returns."

"I think I'm beginning to get the drift now," I told Pickles.

"About time," he said dismissively. "When the first guy comes back, the restaurant man—as the grifters have hoped—keeps the business card in his pocket and tries to buy the fiddle. Its owner hems and haws, and the restaurateur keeps on jacking up his offer until the guy finally sells him the worthless fiddle, for cash on the spot. Chances are, the mark had to empty the till for the dough."

"And of course the first guy never comes back to the restaurant, right?"

"I can't say that you're a quick learner, but now you've got it," Pickles said. "Anyway, that's what Benny was known for, along with running a few other short-cons like three-card monte, the shell game, and the pigeon drop."

"I won't ask you to describe those just now," I told him.

"Good, because I don't have all day to give you lessons in the fine art of grifting," he replied. "Let's just say that some years back, Benny ran out of luck and got nailed by the law while running one of his many cons. He has more or less gone straight since he got out of stir, and he shuns the limelight."

"I won't ask you what 'more or less' means."

"Let's put it this way: Benny didn't cost me a farthing on this business because he owes me a couple of favors—big ones," Pickles said, "but I'm certainly expecting some consideration for services rendered from you."

"I hear you, and be assured that consideration will indeed be given," I told him. He started to squawk that he had expected a more concrete response from me, but I lied about being right up against a deadline and hung up the phone.

I sat staring at the blank plywood wall for several minutes after Pickles' call, contemplating a next move. I could go to the bar on Wilson Avenue myself and take a gander at Whitnauer for myself, maybe even trying to engage him in conversation. Or I could call Fergus Fahey and dump this information in his lap. I was torn, and in the end, I opted for the latter course, in part because of all the times Catherine had urged me to stop acting like I was some sort of rogue avenger, operating like a copper without a badge.

"Is he on the premises?" I asked Elsie Dugo Cascio when she picked up the phone and chirped "Chief Fahey's office."

"He just got back from a meeting with Commissioner Prendergast, and he's in an even more foul mood than usual. Am I to assume that this important?"

"It truly is, you vision of loveliness. You can tell him that I chose to call him rather than to take the law into my own hands."

"I'll relay the message."

"What in the hell is this 'taking the law into your own hands' crap about?" Fahey bellowed when he came on the line.

"I just made a command decision to stop playing hero, which should please you. I think I have the identity of the man who we're calling 'Sam White,' you know, the one who—"

"Yes, I know who you're talking about! Well, spit it out. Let's have it."

I proceeded to give the chief chapter and verse, including the name and address of the Wilson Avenue saloon, which Pickles had supplied to me.

"Very interesting," he snarled. "And just how did you happen to come by this little nugget of information?"

"Somebody I know thinks that he might have seen White, or rather Whitnauer, going into a bar in Uptown."

"And how, pray tell, did this 'somebody' know what Mr. Whitnauer looks like? We haven't released the sketch to the newspapers—unless of course one somehow fell into your hands," Fahey said in a tone laced with sarcasm.

"Fergus, isn't the important thing here that we've got a bead on Whitnauer? Does anything else really matter? And since I've passed along to you what may turn out to be valuable information, I'd like something in return."

"What?"

"Has he, Whitnauer, been spotted going into the fair since that sketch got distributed?"

"Come on, Snap, think for a second. If he were seen, do you think he'd still be on the loose?"

"Good point."

"But," Fahey went on, "I will tell you this, off the record. Three visitors to the fair have been stopped and interrogated. To the ticket-sellers, they looked enough like the drawing of White, or Whitnauer, that they were detained. One was a guy with a mustache and crew cut from Medinah, Ohio, another was a man with his family from someplace in Iowa, and the third was a writer for a railroad fan magazine doing an article about the fair. He was really pissed off at us and threatened to sue somebody."

"I can believe it. Those journalism types can be a pretty dog-gone surly lot. Well, good luck with Mr. Whitnauer."

He growled. "Snap, when all of this is over, by God, you and I are going to have a very long talk."

"I look forward to that."

"I'll just bet you do!" he bellowed for the second time in the conversation, slamming down the phone.

So I had done my civic duty and turned information over to the law. Feeling self-righteous, I dialed the *Tribune* morgue and got Hazel on the second ring.

"Believe it or not, Snap, I was just about to call you," she said.

"I'll bet you say that to all the boys."

"Only the ones I really like, and especially those who remember what I like to drink. It took me longer that I thought to assemble the clips you wanted. I kept getting interrupted by reporters needing information. The nerve of them!"

"I'll say. Some people have no consideration. Was there a lot?"

"Tons. It'll take you a while to wade through all of it. I'll admit I wasn't terribly discriminating, but I felt that when in doubt, I should let you decide if a story had value."

"I like that line of thinking. I'll stop by the Tower after work and pick up the stuff."

CHAPTER THIRTY-ONE

When I got home that night, I was toting a stuffed manila folder.

"Just what do have we here?" Catherine asked after we had embraced. "Homework, perhaps?"

"Of a sort," I said, giving her a partial summary of the day's activities and the contents of the bulging folder.

"Steven Douglas Malek," she said, hands on hips and head cocked, "I thought that you had agreed to stop playing private detective and leave that sort of thing to Chief Fahey and his army."

"There is a thin line, my love, between private eye and investigative reporter."

"A line that you seem to be skating on both sides of, I might add. At the risk of throwing cold water on your enthusiasm, I should point out that you are not at the moment an investigative reporter, but rather a feature writer."

"You have cut me to the very quick, oh, dearest one. Inside every newspaperman, regardless of his title or assignment of the moment, beats the noble heart of an intrepid journalist, on a never-ending quest to right wrongs and pursue an unerring course of justice and truth."

"A very nice speech indeed, sir. I would consider myself chagrined if I truly thought that I had wronged you. However, I remain suspicious."

"I must tell you," I said as we walked to the dinner table, "that I really do pay heed to what you say. Something else transpired today that I didn't tell you about."

"Oh?"

I proceeded to relate my decision not to visit the bar in Uptown that Whitnauer patronized, but rather to turn all my information over to Fergus Fahey and his vast legion of plainclothes foot soldiers.

"I must admit that is progress of a sort," she said as we tackled our roast chicken, mashed potatoes, and peas. "But what's with all the clippings you've brought home? That sounds to me an awful lot like police work in the guise of 'research.'"

"Look, as you know, I have a lot of admiration for Fahey and his leadership. But the Police Department in general, and the Detective Bureau in particular, tend to do things by the numbers, and they sometimes need an injection of imagination and creativity."

"That has an air of superiority about it," Catherine said, raising an eyebrow.

"Maybe, but take today for example: If I hadn't enlisted Pickles Podgorny and his 'irregular' troops, we—and the police—would not have known the identity of the man who very well may be behind all of the fair killings."

"You still don't know if that's really the one, though."

"True enough, but at least it's a start of sorts. And maybe one or more of those clippings I brought home will further help things along."

"I still think you may be taking what Walt Disney said too seriously."

"You mean about someone possibly holding a long-time grudge against the railroads?"

"Yes. That sounds like the plot for a motion picture."

I laughed. "Well, I suppose Disney would readily plead guilty to that charge. After all, he makes movies, albeit animated ones, and he very likely thinks up a lot of their wild and wacky plots. It's possible that he just can't turn off that fertile brain of his."

Catherine joined in the laughter, and after we had washed and dried the dinner dishes, she retreated to her favorite chair in the living room to read "The Way West" by A.B. Guthrie while I sat at the dining room table and started in on the large batch of clips that had been assembled by Hazel.

She had done a thorough job, going back even farther than I had suggested. Interestingly, two of the earliest clippings she included were about rail disasters that had taken place in western Indiana, close to Chicago.

The worst and most famous of these was the 1918 collision near Hammond, just across the state line from Illinois, in which a Hegenbeck-Wallace Circus train got smashed in the rear by another train, whose engineer had fallen asleep at the throttle of his locomotive. Eighty-six were killed, most of them circus personnel, including performers.

There also was a collision in the small town of Porter in 1921 in which one passenger train ploughed into another at a cross-over of two lines, killing thirty-seven. The engineer of one of the trains was found to be at fault for having ignored a red signal.

I spent a long time reading and re-reading the brittle, faded clippings of these two historic wrecks, mulling over whether someone who lost loved ones in one of them might now be exacting revenge on railroads in general. I finally set the articles aside, figuring that because a full generation or more had elapsed since their occurrence, anyone seeking retribution would have long since acted.

A more likely possibility was the April 1946 Naperville, Illinois, train wreck, which I had covered for the *Trib*. In that case, one Burlington Route passenger train bound for the West rammed into the rear of another one that had stopped, shredding the rear coach. Forty-five were killed, with more than one-hundred others injured.

The engineer of the second train, W.W. Blaine, initially was seen as the one causing the crash, but six months later, according to the clips, a DuPage County Grand Jury "blamed the wreck on a series of unconnected negligent activities by both the railroad and the crews" of the two trains. How many people whose relatives died in that tragedy might have reason to get revenge on either the Burlington or railroads as a whole, I wondered.

Then I pulled out a batch of clippings held together by a rubber band that set me to wondering anew. The first article reported on a 1939 mishap on Chicago's Southwest Side. Under the headline THREE BOYS ON BIKES KILLED RACING TRAIN, the Page Three story recounted how eleven-year-old boys on bicycles pedaled along a street that crossed the Rock Island Lines and raced a freight train to the crossing that was moving at "approximately thirty miles per hour."

The boys skirted around the lowered crossing gates and, according to eyewitnesses including the engineer, rode onto the tracks as the steam locomotive blew its whistle repeatedly and slammed on its brakes.

The locomotive struck all three boys, however. One was killed by the impact with the train while the other two were thrown through the air and died instantly of wounds suffered when they hit the street.

Another clipping, dated a few days later, reported that a coroner's jury ruled that the deaths were accidental, although parents of two of the boys claimed that the engineer had not made a great enough effort to stop. They had disrupted the proceedings with shouts and threats against the engineer.

Yet another clipping, dated a few months later, was a one-paragraph item that said the engineer, Josef Schneider, had quit his job as a Rock Island engineer because of what was referred to as "a state of deep depression" over the accident.

The fourth and final article in the batch that Hazel had bundled together for me was the obituary of Schneider, age fifty-six, in October 1942. He had hanged himself in the basement of the family home on South Sawyer Avenue. There was no mention of a suicide note.

I had of course been a reporter on the *Tribune* during these years, but somehow this story had eluded me, other than a vague recollection I had of the accident. I wanted to know more about the star-crossed Mr. Schneider, and I knew just who to ask.

CHAPTER THIRTY-TWO

The next morning I left the house almost an hour earlier than usual, first destination: Tribune Tower, to return the clippings that had been assembled for me. The paper, and by extension, the morgue, had a rule that clips under no circumstances were to be taken from the building, and the last thing I wanted to do was to get Hazel in trouble. So it was that at 8:35, I placed the envelope in her hands with profuse thanks, then passed through the local room, waving to a few colleagues whom I rarely saw and stopping to give my regards to Day City Editor Hal Murray.

Back in the fair's press room, where I remained the only occupant, I thumbed through the bulky Chicago phone directory and found the name I wanted: Zack Yeager.

Zack had been an intrepid *Trib* police reporter for more than thirty years before retiring in the early 1940s. Not only was he a tiger once he got onto the scent of a story, he also had a memory that rivaled that of my wife Catherine's late father, the legendary City News Bureau reporter Lemuel "Steel Trap" Bascomb.

"Yeager at this end," he answered in a gravelly tone on the second ring.

"Hello Zack, this is a ghost from your past."

"I'm pretty good with voices, and I've gotta say this sounds a hell of a lot like the one and only Steve 'Snap' Malek, boy reporter. How'm I doing?"

"As good as ever, Zack. What's going on with you these days?"

"Arthritis, for one thing, but that's not about to stop me from getting out to Sportsman's and Hawthorne to watch the ponies run and put down a small wager now and again."

"Are you winning?"

"Now and again."

"Do you miss the exciting world of the daily deadlines?"

"You know, I did at first, Snap. The first year after I left was really tough, actually tougher on Maggie than on me, because I was such a bear around the house, a real pain in the butt. If she had bumped me off then, any jury would have ruled it justifiable homicide."

I laughed. "It couldn't have been that bad now, Zack."

"It was pretty bad, but then I adjusted. It helps that the grandkids are nearby. Our daughter Amy lives in Evergreen Park, so we see them all pretty often. And then there's Sportsman's and Hawthorne, as I mentioned. But how about you? Bring me up to date."

"Right now, the paper has me doing feature stuff out at the Railroad Fair."

"Oh yeah, come to think of it, I've seen a few of your bylines. Some strange things happening out there, eh?"

"I'll say. Before I get back to the fair, on a personal note, you may know that I got divorced a few years back."

"Yeah, I think that I had heard that someplace. Sorry to hear it."

"Don't be. The story has a happy ending. I'm married again, and I like to think I'm a better man this time around. My wife is Steel Trap Bascomb's daughter."

"I'll be damned! I'll be goddamned! Good for you, Snap. Now ol' Steel Trap, *there* was a man. We'll never see his likes again."

"Yeah, and although I had met him a few times in earlier years, I really got acquainted with him toward the end, which is how I met Catherine. Of course by then his mind was going, but he still had moments when the old brilliance showed through."

"God, I remember one time when he and I covered a fatal down near the Stockyards in '21 or '22, I think. The stiff had been trying to rob a little ma and pa store and got outdrawn by the grocer, who plugged him as he was pulling out his own gun. We walked in, and Steel Trap must have been at least thirty feet away from the body, which was lying face down on the floor of the store, when he said 'That's Two-Bits Tomassini, I'd know him anywhere.'

"When I asked where he had run into this Two-Bits character before, he told me it was back in 1907, when he was covering the courts, that they had hauled Tomassini in for kiting checks. A minor thing like that fifteen years before, and damned if Steel Trap didn't remember it—even the month in '07 when it happened, April!"

"Incredible story, Zack."

"Yeah., but I have a feeling you didn't call up just to hear me reminisce about the great old days chasing down stories and finding ways to screw the opposition out of scoops."

"I recall that you've got a damned good memory yourself."

"Nothin' like Steel Trap, though. Like I said, with him, they threw away the mold."

"Well, let me test you, if you don't mind. Do you happen to remember a railroad engineer named Josef Schneider?"

I could hear a deep exhale at the other end. "Oh, yeah, Snap, I remember very well, too well. A sad, sad story. Does this have anything to do with that Railroad Fair of yours?"

"Maybe, but I'm not sure. Tell me about Schneider."

"Well, do you know about the three kids who got hit by his train?"

"Yeah, I do now. I vaguely remember when it happened, but my own memory got a jogging when I read the clips yesterday about the whole business, including the inquest and the suicide. Can you fill in some blanks for me?"

"A few of them, anyway. I was at the inquest, and it was nasty, Snap, I mean really nasty. The parents of these kids were damned near out of control, particularly when the deaths got ruled an accident."

"They thought that he should have been able to stop the train, is that it?"

"Yeah, but others who were on the scene said that was impossible; the train was going too fast. The kids apparently had waited until the last possible moment to race in front of the engine. It sounds like they were playing some sort of 'chicken.'"

"Well, it also sounds like it pretty well ended Schneider's life, too."

"Yes, you're absolutely right. It didn't help matters that he was a German immigrant who spoke with a heavy accent. There was still a lot of residual resentment of Germans from the First War in a lot of neighborhoods, as you know, and there were more bad feelings by the late '30s, what with Hitler on the scene by then."

"That all adds up to a formula for trouble," I said.

"Sure does, and the trouble started right there at the inquest. After the 'accident' verdict, the kids' parents shouted things like 'Dirty Kraut' and 'You bloody damned Heinie.' Somebody even called him a Nazi, which of course made no sense whatever. The bailiff and a couple of cops had to clear the room. The screaming continued in the hall and even out on the street."

"I gather the hatred followed the poor bastard for the rest of his life."

"You gather right. I didn't follow what happened next real closely—I had a lot of other stuff to keep me busy at the time—but I do know that Schneider left the Rock Island just to get away from all the hassle he was getting, not only from the parents of the dead kids but from their neighbors as well. They all made him a scapegoat for what happened."

"Then what?"

"After a year or so, he tried to get his old job back, but apparently the Rock Island was worried about his mental condition, possibly with some justification, and they turned him down cold. After that, he tried to catch on with several other railroads in the area, I think the Santa Fe, the C&EI, the Monon, the Milwaukee Road, and maybe even a few others, too. I'm fuzzy on the details.

"But it was no dice. Apparently the word had gotten around the railroads that he was unstable. Also, or so the story went at the time, these other lines were worried that if they hired him, they'd catch all manner of crap from the families of those kids."

"Sort of an informal blackball, wasn't it?"

"Yeah, that's a good way to put it, and I guess you know the rest."

"The suicide?"

"He hanged himself in the basement of his house. I didn't

go to the funeral, but Don Haggerty did." Zack was referring to a longtime *Trib* police reporter who had died a few years back.

"Did you ever talk to Haggerty about it—the funeral, I mean?"

"I did, because I had been curious about the whole situation over the years. Sort of an American tragedy, you know?"

"Uh-huh. Somebody could sure write a novel about it, all right. Did Haggerty find out anything at the funeral?"

"He talked to the widow, who said her husband's life for the last several years had been a nightmare, that he'd lost weight, started hitting the bottle hard, which according to her he'd never done before. Stuff like that."

"Did Schneider have any kids?"

"Haggerty never said, as far as I can remember. The only other thing I'm sure about is that the widow moved again after her husband's death."

"Tried to disappear, eh?"

"I suppose so," Zack said.

"A lot of lives ruined."

"For sure. Do you figure Schneider's ghost is bumping 'em off out at the Railroad Fair?"

"I'm not quite to that point yet," I said, laughing. "But it's possible there could be some sort of a connection."

"Well, be careful, huh, Snap? I've read about some of your exploits the last few years, and I know that you have a tendency to take chances. Don't go doing anything foolish, now, y'hear?"

"I hear. Good talking to you, Zack, and I'll keep you posted."

CHAPTER THIRTY-THREE

Just as I hung up, a slender and poised auburn-haired woman in a tailored suit whom I guessed to be in her mid-to late-twenties glided gracefully into the room on fashionable high heels.

"Hello. I didn't see any sign on the door. This is the press room, isn't it?" she asked, brushing an errant strand of hair from her forehead.

"You have got the right place," I said with a grin, standing as my mother long ago taught me to do when a woman enters a room.

"I'm Betty Ann Wells of the *Daily News*," she said, offering a hand with a firm grip.

"Nice to meet you, Betty Ann. I'm Steve Malek of the *Tribune*."

"*The* Steve Malek, no less, better known to his friends as 'Snap,' am I right? I must say that I feel most honored."

"No reason to," I told her with a chuckle. "And by all means, call me Snap, which instantly makes you a friend. What brings you to this remote outpost on the fringes of the empire?"

"I'm here to do a feature on one of the girls in the Cypress Gardens Water Show. She was runner-up in the Miss Georgia pageant last year, or so I've been informed."

"I know your byline," I said. "You did that excellent feature a few weeks back about the woman in Evanston who had raised—what was it?—thirteen foster kids over the years."

"It was fourteen, and thanks so much for remembering," she said. "I guess we all often wonder if anybody actually reads what we write—and takes note of the byline."

"We do indeed. Well, I was impressed, both by your reporting and by that woman. She was a real inspiration."

"Far more than the girl who I'm going to see today, I'm sure."

"I interviewed one of those pretty water-skiing damsels myself awhile back, and she looked like she could easily have been a Miss Alabama," I told her. "I sincerely hope that your southern belle has more to say than mine did, though."

Betty Ann smiled, showing dimples. "I hope so, too. I understand from the grapevine that you are stationed here for the duration of the fair."

"You heard right. It's sure turned out differently than I figured."

"I'll say! Do you have any thoughts about who's behind all the . . . deaths?"

"A few, but they're pretty vague right at the moment."

"I was surprised when I heard that you'd been assigned here for the summer. Your reputation as a crime reporter is well known all over town, as I know you're aware."

"You flatter me."

"Not really. I'm just stating the obvious. After all, everybody knows you saved the President's life last year, among other things. And I remember when I was in journalism school up at Northwestern reading about how you helped crack those murders surrounding the hush-hush work on the atom bomb at the University of Chicago during the war."

"I really appreciate the kind words," I said with a shrug.

"With your reputation, I was surprised that you got assigned out here."

"To be honest, I was surprised myself, and not exactly happy."

"But now look at how things have turned out. You're right back in the middle of the news again. Adventure must follow you wherever you go."

"So several others have remarked. What's happened here the last few weeks is another surprise that I didn't see coming."

Betty Ann pursed her lips and frowned. "I would give anything to have some kind of hard news beat instead of this fluffy feature stuff. But I'm well aware of how things work on the papers. About the only women in the newsrooms around town are the 'sob sisters,' whose assignments as you know are to cover the biggest trials for murder or divorce and wring every drop of emotion and pathos and drama out of the proceedings," she said with a touch of bitterness.

I nodded. "That's a pretty accurate description. I've got to believe the situation is going to change sometime, though. After all, during the war, women filled quite a few reporting positions on the *Trib*, and on the other papers as well."

She made a face. "Yeah, and then look what happened the minute the war ended: Home came the men, and all the women who had been covering police news, fires, and the like went back to writing feature stories about beauty queens and debutantes and triple-layer chocolate cakes. It's true that once in awhile, somebody more substantial like that Evanston foster mom comes along, but that's been the exception in my experience."

"I still think that better days are coming for the female reporters," I told her, only partially believing my words.

"Well, I have to admit there is one advantage to being a woman on the paper, although even that is kind of insulting."

"Oh?"

"When I left the office to come down here, my editor—who's a woman—said to me, 'take a cab and expense it. I don't want you riding down there on a street car or a bus.' Do you know how the male reporters on the *Daily News* travel?"

"If it's like at the *Tribune,* they go by said street car or bus."

"Yeah, or the Elevated if that's more convenient. But all of us poor little gals have to be protected, you know."

"Maybe that will change someday, too."

"I hope you're right. I—" She was interrupted by the arrival in the press room of a smiling and over-eager Fred Metzger.

"Ah, Miss Wells of the *Daily News*, right?" he said, introducing himself, bowing, and thrusting out a hand. "I am so glad that you're here. Sorry that I wasn't out at the front gate to meet you, but I got tied up. Are you ready to go and meet Holly Webster?"

"I am indeed," she said, nodding curtly and whipping a reporter's notebook out of her purse. "Lead the way."

"I think you will find the young lady charming, absolutely charming," Metzger gushed. "Almost as charming as you are."

As they were leaving, Betty Ann looked back at me over one shoulder and rolled her eyes. I got the message.

CHAPTER THIRTY-FOUR

About twenty minutes after leaving with Betty Ann, Metzger returned to the press room.

"Ah, did you get the lovely Miss Wells hooked up with the lovely Miss What's-Her-Name from down Georgia way?" I asked.

The PR man grinned. "Holly Webster. I did indeed, and they truly are an attractive pair to behold together. Miss Wells herself could certainly have been a beauty queen, don't you think?"

"Okay, enough," I said, holding up a hand. "Stop your drooling, Metzger, and tell me what you've got for in store for me today."

"Ah yes, of course," he said, consulting papers on his ever-present clipboard. "There's a whole group, more than a hundred in all, of retired employees of the New York Central Railroad and their families who have come by train—on the New York Central, of course—from the East to see the fair and tour the city for a few days. I thought that you might find it interesting to spend time with them."

I shot him a look, and I wasn't smiling. "Think this'll be any better than that three-generation family of colossal bores from Indiana that you hooked me up with?"

Metzger laughed nervously. "Well for one thing, there are a lot more folks in this group. Somebody's really bound to be interesting."

"I suppose so, given the law of averages, but what if I have to work my way through all one-hundred of these pensioners and their loving spouses before I find the one fascinating story in the lot? It could end up taking all week."

That stopped Metzger, who allowed a woebegone expression to take over his face, if only for a moment. "Afraid that's the best I can do at the moment, Snap. I have to be honest; I'm running out of ideas for you. It's hard coming up with something, or someone, fresh every day."

I sympathized with the rotund PR man and took pity on him. "I think your initial excitement at having a reporter for a Chicago daily here every day has changed to a frustration. It's like having to constantly feed a beast," I said, "and I happen to be the beast. Tell you what: I'll meet with this bunch from the—what was it—New York Central? Who knows, maybe something will present itself."

As it turned out, very little presented itself, although I did find a couple named Phelps who had lived in eleven different towns in Upstate New York and Ohio over the course of forty-five years. Calvin Phelps had been a station agent for the railroad, and he and his wife, Sylvia, were childless.

"Cal and me, we both always just liked change," the well-padded Sylvia told me with a sweet smile, bright blue eyes twinkling behind bifocals rimless. "Almost every time the opportunity came up for him to work in another town along the main line, we took it."

"'Course we never bought a house, always rented," he said, passing a hand over a full head of white hair and grinning. "But that was okay because I wasn't all that interested in being a homeowner anyway. Never liked the idea of being tied down."

"What was your favorite place in all those years?" I asked.

"I dunno," he said, turning to his spouse. "I liked 'em all, but I suppose maybe that would be Batavia, eh, Syl?"

"Batavia was nice," she agreed, bobbing her head, "although I think for me it was Palmyra, where we stayed six years and made so many friends. We had such a nice minister there, too, Reverend Hawkins, who gave those inspirational sermons that made you want to rush right out and change the world. We're Methodists, always have been. But when he got transferred to another church someplace down in Pennsylvania, we pushed on, too."

"Now you're retired and don't move around anymore, I suppose."

"Now there you are wrong, young man," Sylvia Phelps said, gently shaking a finger at me. "We decided to retire in Canastota because several trains a day stop there. Cal has a lifetime pass on the NYC for both of us, and he and I are always off visiting the nice friends we made in the places where we lived all along the line. Many times, we even stay overnight with these folks, and they seem happy to have us."

"And we still don't own a house," her husband said with pride. "Shoot, we even took the train all the way to New York City one time. I had to see the Grand Central Terminal once before I died, and it was worth it. Ever been there?"

I shook my head. "Great place, you've just got to make the trip someday," he said. "You'll never forget it."

I promised that I would and we parted. So I got my story that day after all. Something of an American saga. To cap it off, Phil Muller showed up and took a shot of the oft-traveled couple. When I was back in the press room typing and then dictating the Phelps's nomadic tale, Betty Ann Wells of the *Daily News* returned, slumping into the chair at her newspaper's desk with a protracted groan, kicking off her patent-leather pumps, and wiggling her toes.

"Well, Miss Betty, how did your session with our Georgian beauty go?" I asked.

"She is beautiful, absolutely no question about that. Just being around her made me feel dumpy."

"Now there I insist on drawing the line. I simply cannot imagine anyone making you feel dumpy under any circumstances."

"Well thank you for that, Mr. Snap Malek. You are a throwback to the lost days of gallantry. Back to the interview: I'm afraid it was a lot like the way you described your session with the Alabama girl. Don't get me wrong; Miss Holly Webster is a very proper young lady who knows how to water ski extremely well, but she does not have a lot to say, other than how much she loves Georgia and all of those wonderful people back home. I could almost smell the magnolias and visualize the peach trees and see Scarlett O'Hara's plantation when she talked."

"Sounds familiar. But you've got yourself enough for a piece?"

She threw up her hands and let them drop into her lap. "Oh, I suppose so, and our photographer took a whole slew of shots of her. One is almost sure to run with the story tomorrow. We never miss a chance at getting some cheesecake into print, you know, like all the other papers in town, including your own."

"Definitely including my own," I concurred, leaning back and lighting up a Lucky. "So it sounds like you can call the day at least a qualified success."

"I guess so. Do you mind if I ask you a business question?"

"Not at all."

"Do you think there's any chance that the *Trib* would ever hire me as something other than a feature writer?"

"You're talking about the news side, right?"

"Of course."

"There's always a chance, but—"

"But not much of one?"

"Well, we've got far and away the biggest newsroom staff of any paper in town, so if things eventually do open up for more women, the *Tribune* is most likely to be the place where it opens up first."

"That doesn't sound very encouraging."

"Sorry, but to be honest, I don't see anything happening in the near-range future. Maybe someday, though . . ."

She nodded somberly and turned to the sturdy Underwood on the desk marked DAILY NEWS, where she began transcribing the notes on her labored interview with the lovely water skier who had almost become Miss Georgia.

More than a decade was to pass before Betty Ann Wells, who went on to make a name for herself as a *Daily News* feature writer, joined the *Tribune*, first as a general assignment reporter, then as a foreign correspondent, first in London and later Paris. It was when she was stationed in the latter city that she ventured into Algeria, reporting on that North African land's war of independence from France. Her coverage there would win her a Pulitzer Prize.

CHAPTER THIRTY-FIVE

With the Phelps story behind me, I reached for the phone and dialed a familiar number. Elsie answered on the first ring, as usual, and put me straight through to Fergus Fahey.

"What now?" he asked in his familiar world-weary voice.

"Just checking in. I realize how much you miss me."

"Miss you? How could I miss you? You're on the blasted horn to me every time I take a deep breath or light a cigarette. It's like you never left the building. Next thing, you'll be showing up in my dreams—or should I say nightmares?"

"I notice that you always manage to take my calls, though."

"That's because I'm terrified you've gotten yourself into another one of your patented jams and that we'll have to get you out of it somehow."

"Well, I admit that I'm not completely jam-proof, but that's not the reason for this call. I'm wondering whether you've gotten hold of the elusive Mr. Whitnauer yet."

"Hell, no. We've had men, different men, visit that seedy bar in Uptown every night, and the bastard hasn't shown up."

"Maybe he's been tipped off somehow and is lying low."

"Or maybe this whole business is a wild goose chase, one that you've helped get us into."

"Maybe it is, but somebody is killing people out here, and it seems likely that it's the so-called Whitnauer. Unless, of course, you've got your eye on somebody else who you're not bothering to tell me about."

"As much as it might come as a shock, I don't tell you everything I know. But in this case, we're nowhere—off the record as usual, of course."

"What next?"

"How in blazes do I know? Obviously, we'll keep on trying to find this Whitnauer, if he's even still in Chicago."

"Well, for what it's worth, I'm pulling for you, Fergus."

"Swell," he said sourly. "That knowledge alone will keep me going."

I replaced the receiver in its cradle, leaned back in my chair, put my feet up on the desk, and lit a Lucky Strike. I'd taken two puffs when the phone rang and I picked up the receiver without identifying myself.

"Mr. Stephen Malek? A female voice said over static.

"Yes, speaking."

"Long distance call, hold on please. I have your party, sir," she said, obviously to the caller.

"Hello, am I talking to Mr. Steve Malek?" a voice crackled over the wires.

"You are indeed."

"Walt Disney at this end. How are you, sir?"

"Fine, just fine, Mr. Disney. Good to hear from you."

"Your Mr. Murray at the *Tribune* very kindly gave me this number. I am telephoning you for two reasons, first to thank you for that very gracious story in your newspaper about Ward Kimball and me at the Railroad Fair. Some old family friends in Chicago mailed me the clipping. It's nice to be remembered in the town where one spent a lot of growing-up time."

"It was my pleasure, both meeting you and writing the article, Mr. Disney."

"Now the second reason for my call: I am extremely curious about what's been happening at your fair since we left. On the way back to California on the Super Chief, I gave a great deal of thought to the deaths you've had there. Along, of course, with plans for the amusement park I told you about. Has there been any more trouble?"

"Sadly, yes." I told him about the man found floating in the lake, Alec Cunningham, and how all indications pointed to murder.

"That so?" the filmmaker said. "I didn't see anything about it in print out here, but then, I'm afraid that our papers are notorious for being very parochial, very local in scope. May I assume that no one is in custody?"

"You assume correctly. The police have a line on one man, but they have not been able to find him yet, at least as of yesterday." I then went on to tell Disney my theory about how the Schneider saga of years ago might well be the genesis of what now was occurring at the fair.

"That's very interesting, and it supports the original comment I made that these fairground deaths may have been because of a long-standing grudge held against a railroad or railroads. May I make a suggestion to you, Mr. Malek?"

"Please, by all means."

"Let me preface it by saying that I have been often accused—by Ward Kimball among many others—of having an overactive imagination. Ward says that I am prone to 'flights of fancy,' as he calls them, so you may want to take what I say with that proverbial grain of salt."

"Fair enough, Mr. Disney."

"All right then, here we go. I'm sorry to say this, but it seems to me that your man is almost sure to strike again. Do you happen to know the date on which that accident happened, the one where those boys were killed?"

"No, but I can easily find out."

"By all means I suggest that you do so, as soon as possible. It is entirely possible that your man will commit his biggest crime of all on the anniversary of that very day, if by chance that happens to come during the run of the fair."

"Hmm. As long as you are indulging in what Ward Kimball calls 'flights of fancy', do you have any suggestion as to what form that crime will take?"

"I have been thinking a good deal about that as well. If I really desired to create the maximum amount of havoc at your city's wonderful homage to railroading, I would stage something truly spectacular, specifically a derailment."

"Oh, you must mean on one of those historic trains that goes across the stage in the pageant?"

"No, sir, I said a *maximum* amount of havoc, which means loss of life, possibly in sizeable numbers, Mr. Malek. Few people would likely be harmed if one of the slow-moving pageant engines left the rails."

"True. I don't know what that leaves then," I told him.

"Of course you do—it's obvious! The Deadwood Central Railroad, that wonderful frontier line that runs the full length of the fairgrounds, with those 19th century western steam locomotives and open-air passenger cars, cars with a lot of the visitors jammed into them. Just think what could happen if one of those trains left the rails and tipped over, or worse yet, rolled over."

"With all due respect, that seems pretty far-fetched," I said.

He chuckled. "Well, Mr. Malek, I told you that I've been accused of possessing an overactive imagination. It comes from helping to dream up those wild and wondrous movie plots, I suppose. Anyway, you can do with this as you please. I suppose the police would dismiss the theory out of hand."

"Very possibly. But you've given me something to think about."

"Good. I would be very pleased to learn from you how all of this plays out."

"I will be sure to let you know, Mr. Disney. I really appreciate your interest." He gave me his private telephone line at the studio.

Seconds after I hung up, I dialed the number of the *Tribune's* morgue. Hazel answered.

"I have a small favor, oh blessed lady of the archives."

"Fire away, buster."

"Would you be so kind as to check one of those clips you pulled together for me? It's that sad story about the three boys who were killed by a freight train on the South Side back in 1939. I need to know the exact date it happened. I should have written it down, of course, but I didn't."

"Well, shame on you," Hazel chided. "I'll be right with you." She probably was gone no more than ninety seconds, but it seemed like a week before she came back on the line. "I've got it right here, Snap. August 4, 1939."

Today was August 2nd.

CHAPTER THIRTY-SIX

So now what? I lifted myself from the old wooden desk chair and stepped out into the splendid early afternoon. The sky was cloudless, the sun was warm, but not too warm, and a gentle breeze wafted in off the tranquil waters of Lake Michigan, where the white sails of pleasure craft stood in sharp contrast to the flat blue backdrop. An idyllic Chicago postcard scene, a perfect August day.

I strolled the grounds, mulling my options, none of which was appealing. After a swing through the Indian pueblo village, the New Orleans street scene, and the Florida tropical gardens, I made my decision and headed for the front gate.

The taxi ride to 11th and State took ten minutes. Once inside the Headquarters building, I took the elevator straight to the third floor and Fergus Fahey's office. There would not be any "hi-there-old-comrades" social visit to the press room one flight farther up.

"Well, if it isn't himself in the very flesh!" Elsie bubbled, clapping her hands. "To what do we owe this surprise visit?"

"Ah, fair lady, above all else I wanted to see your smiling face of course. But I also took a chance that he might be available."

"He's within, and as crotchety as ever," she said, tilting her head in the direction of the closed door to his office.

"Is he by any chance expecting anyone—such as my esteemed colleague Mr. Westcott of the *Tribune*? Because I would prefer not to run into that particular gentleman. This is strictly a confidential visit."

"Mr. Westcott was here late this morning, as usual. Much later, by the way, than you used to come down," she said, waving a hand as if to dismiss Ken Westcott from further discussion. "Now, let me see if I can squeeze you in. A friend here to see you," she mouthed into the intercom.

"I've told you before, I don't have any friends," the voice squawked. "Whoever it is, they enter at their peril."

"Peril my foot," I said, stepping into his office. "Yet here I am, a friend bearing gifts." I lobbed a just-opened pack of Lucky Strikes onto his blotter and dropped into one of the two battered and unmatched desk chairs.

"My God, have they given you your old job back now?" Fahey asked, rooting in the cigarette pack.

"Sorry to disappoint, but I am still out there along our beautiful coast, along with all those locomotives and ice skaters and water skiers and Indians. But I need to talk, and it is very important."

"It seems like you and I have been talking every day, sometimes more than once a day," the chief growled as he lit up a Lucky. "Why bother making the trip over here when you can just harass me by telephone?"

I leaned forward, elbows on his desk. "Fergus, you have known me for a long time, and I think you will agree that I am not easily alarmed, and I am by no means a crackpot. A pest—maybe sometimes—but a crackpot, never."

"So stipulated," he said, narrowing his eyes. "What comes next?"

I lit up a Lucky from the pack myself. "I wouldn't have come over here in person and to take up your valuable time if I wasn't worried. Make that *very* worried."

"Get to the point, will you!"

"I'm scared shitless that something bad, and I mean terribly bad, is going to happen at the Railroad Fair this week, specifically Thursday."

He ran a hand through his hair. "I would say that plenty of terribly bad stuff has already happened out there."

"True, but I think something even worse is coming." I mentioned the case of the three boys who were killed by the train by way of a preface.

"Yeah, I remember that awful business," Fahey said, shaking his head. "So, what makes this week so special?"

"As I've told you before, I've got this feeling that whoever—presumably our Mr. Whitnauer—is behind the fair killings is doing it to get revenge on the railroads overall."

"So you have said, but I still think it sounds far-fetched."

I then told him about what had happened to Josef Schneider in the years following the accident, ending with his suicide.

Fahey ground out one half-smoked cigarette and lit another. "At the risk of repeating myself, so what?"

"What I think is that this Whitnauer character is probably a relative of Schneider, maybe even a son or a nephew or a brother, and that he's never forgiven the railroads for the way they treated old Josef, what with several of the lines refusing to hire him after a tragedy that wasn't even really his fault."

"I still say far-fetched."

"Think about it, Fergus. From what my old *Trib* colleague Zack Yeager recalls—and he has an incredible memory as I'm sure you know—Schneider was turned down by a whole lot of railroads even though his work record had been good up to the time of the accident. So I think that our man Whitnauer is taking it out on the whole lot of them. There's been a killing at the pageant, at the Illinois Central exhibit, at the Rio Grande 'tunnel', and at the water show put on by a bunch of railroads serving the South. It seems that our killer has been lashing out indiscriminately."

Fahey rubbed his chin. "Are you thinking this Whitnauer is related to Schneider, like maybe his son?"

"Could be," I said. "If Schneider were alive, he'd be about sixty-three, and from the descriptions, Whitnauer looks to be in his forties."

"So, to repeat myself, why do you think something is going to happen this particular week?"

I wasn't about to tell Fahey that the theory had been put forth by Walt Disney, or he would have kicked me out of his office and slammed the door behind me. As it was, the whole business did indeed seem implausible. But I pushed on.

"Because the anniversary of the accident is this Thursday. The tenth anniversary. I have this hunch that Whitnauer plans to kill a whole slew of people this time."

"Go on," Fahey said cautiously, coming forward in his chair. At least I had his attention now.

I took a deep breath. "Okay, here goes. The best way to hurt the maximum number of people at the fair is to sabotage the old-time train—it's called the Deadwood Central—that carries people along a track from one end of the fairgrounds to the other. A hundred or more on every ride, packed into these open-sided excursion cars."

"You mean this . . . Whitnauer loony would dynamite the train?" Fahey said, throwing up his hands in disbelief.

"Probably not dynamite it," I told him. "More likely, he would do something else to cause it to derail, like somehow mess with the tracks. As I said, those passenger cars are probably full on just about every trip. Even though the old train likely doesn't go more than about thirty miles an hour or so, you can imagine what would happen if that whole damn thing left the tracks and the cars rolled over."

He made a face. "It sounds to me like a third-rate movie plot."

"I won't argue the point, but look at what's happened at this fair already this summer. Whoever would have predicted that?"

"Yeah, but you don't have any idea if the crap that's been going on out there has anything to do with this Schneider business. There's no evidence whatever of a connection," Fahey said. "Besides, it's possible that Whitnauer, if that's really his name, has left town, or at least stopped hanging out at that saloon up on Wilson Avenue."

"Fergus, would you be willing to swear that he hasn't been back at the fair, maybe even multiple times, since the shooting?"

"Just what is that supposed to mean?"

"Let's be realistic. How many people go through the gates every day? Twenty thousand? Thirty? Forty? Also, the girls manning the ticket windows are practically kids. Would you trust them to spot a man they've seen in a sketch, a man who may have drastically altered his appearance?"

"Some of my men are at those gates every day, too," he snapped.

"Okay, granted, but you told me yourself that several people have gotten stopped and questioned because somebody thought they might be Whitnauer. After you've made a few mistakes like that, the tendency of a cop or a fair employee is to back off for fear of embarrassing visitors—and yourself as well. That's simply human nature. I say that if the man wants to get into the grounds badly enough, he will. Besides, it's entirely possible he could even wade in from the east through the shallow water at night. The fair hasn't got the lake fenced off."

"You're really reaching now, Snap," Fahey said, shaking his head.

"Oh, yeah, I suppose I am. But you haven't found Whitnauer, and the deaths have kept happening. Seems like if you're going to err, it should be on the side of caution."

Fahey lit yet another Lucky and frowned, but it seemed like he was considering what I had said. "So you say the anniversary of those kids' deaths is the day after tomorrow?"

"Yes, August 4th."

"All right, I'm going to have some conversations. In the meantime, you are going to keep everything that was just said in this room off the record. Do I make myself clear?"

"Perfectly. Then what?"

"Then we'll see," he murmured, suddenly calm. In all the years I have known him, I've never been sure which Fergus Fahey I was more comfortable with: The one who vented and turned red or the one who clammed up and wore a poker face. In truth, I was more comfortable with the former version because I knew just where I stood.

"Well, I should get back to the fair," I told him. "Let me know if there's anything I can do, or anything I should know. Remember, as I've said before, I can be among your eyes and ears at the fair."

"Right," he answered absently, swiveling around and looking out the window. I said good-by to his broad back and left.

CHAPTER THIRTY-SEVEN

The time has almost come, Papa. On Thursday, exactly ten years will have passed. At last, your spirit will be able to rest in peace. Everything is almost in order. It will come after dark, and it will make news, lots of news, both here and across the country, maybe even across the world.

Afterward, I will send messages to all of the local newspapers and the radio stations and the television stations, telling them why all of these things have happened at the fair. Everyone will remember you once again, Papa, and the way you suffered unjustly because of the railroads. This has been the railroads' turn to suffer. Those whose loved ones have suffered and will suffer at the fair will hate the railroads. They will then hate the railroads as I have hated them, Papa . . .

CHAPTER THIRTY-EIGHT

Back at the fair after my session with Fahey, I found it difficult to concentrate, although I had committed to a late afternoon interview with a man who had been dubbed "the world's
greatest rail fan" by one of the railroad enthusiast magazines.
He turned out to be a heavy-set, good-natured fellow of fifty-
five wearing a striped locomotive engineer's cap and a red-and-
yellow Hawaiian-style shirt covered with painted metal pins
bearing the insignias of what he said were "every doggone Class
I railroad there is in the whole of the U.S.A."

This was Millard Wilhelm of Tulsa, Oklahoma. He claimed
to have ridden more than a half-million miles on trains in the
U.S. and twenty-seven other countries and said he had a dozen
photo albums to prove it. I didn't ask to see them.

"Where have you managed to find the time for all of this
world traveling?" I asked Wilhelm as we sat drinking coffee in a
booth at the Railhead Inn on the fairgrounds.

"Well, for one thing, I'm single, always have been," he drawled, stroking his salt-and-pepper goatee. "The other thing is that my daddy, may the Good Lord rest his soul, made himself a whole lot of money in oil. So . . . well, I have never had the need to go to work," he added without the slightest hint of embarrassment.

He went on to describe his most memorable trips, including one through eastern Turkey—Anatolia, as he called it—in which his train was stopped in rugged mountain country by bandits on horseback waving rifles who went through the cars relieving passengers of their money and jewelry.

"Funniest doggone thing, though," Wilhelm drawled with a chuckle. "When they came to me, I pulled out my American passport and held it up, and they backed away, arms in the air like I was holding a gosh-darned gun on them rather than the other way around. One said something like 'mer-i-can' to the others, and they just smiled and bowed and moved on to rob the other folks in the coaches.

"They never got away with a red cent though," he laughed. "Somehow the local lawmen found out what was going on and they came galloping up on their own darn horses, nabbing the bunch of them."

"Interesting. Do you figure the cops in on the whole thing?" I asked.

"Can't say for sure, but I doubt it, because they did return everybody's money and other stuff to them."

If nothing else, I did get a decent light feature out of the afternoon's time, and the affable Mr. Wilhelm kept my mind off more serious matters for an hour or so, regaling me with tales of his other trips. Of course, Phil Muller was on hand to take pictures of "the world's greatest rail fan," even promising to mail him a print of one of the shots at no charge.

"Hey Snap, can't you find some more people to write about like that water-skiing cutie from down in Alabama?" Muller asked after the porky Wilhelm had waddled off to see the "Wheel's-a-Rolling" pageant. "Seems like the last several people you've interviewed have been old or fat or dowdy or worse, all three."

"Sorry to disappoint you, Phil, but I'm afraid the sad fact is that only a small minority of the people on this planet look anything like the young lady of whom you speak," I told him. "Just be happy that you've gotten to spend so much time this summer out here in the sunshine and the blue skies and the cool zephyrs that float in off our beautiful lake."

"Geez, that's almost poetic, Snap," he said, "but I'd still like to get some more cheesecake stuff."

"Okay, here's an idea, you incorrigible old lecher. Get yourself down to the water show, or to that ice ballet on the rink right next door to it, and take a bunch of group shots of some of the young lovelies who are performing. I'll bet anything that whichever picture editor is working today will be delighted to run one of them on the back page with a caption. And just think of the fun you'll have."

"Thanks! I guess I should have thought of that myself."

"Yes, you should have. But there's no charge for the idea."

Muller trotted happily off toward the water and ice shows in search of feminine pulchritude while I returned to my desk in the press room to write about the self-styled world's most-traveled train passenger, who had the photo albums to prove it. After I had finished the piece and dictated it to Thompson on the rewrite desk, I set off in the direction of the Deadwood Central Railroad, which ran along the west edge of the fair, paralleling Lake Shore Drive but separated from it by a high wooden stockade fence that enhanced the Wild West feeling that the railroad sought to create.

Nothing would have shattered that "frontier" image for people riding the vintage train more quickly than a view of the taxis and heavily chromed, sleek postwar automobiles careening along the eight-lane road at well above the posted speed limit.

I walked along beside the Deadwood Central's track, trying to guess where a saboteur intent on a derailment might be expected to strike. First off, I figured that with the ever-earlier sunsets of these late summer days, Whitnauer probably would look for the least-lit stretch of track and wait until after dark to act. He also would choose a place where the train was going the fastest, presumably at about the midway point between the two terminal stations.

Dark and mid-route it should be, then, if I had this figured correctly. The best spot, if I were trying to wreck a train, would be close to the giant Paul Bunyan robot and our new friend Nils Ericsson, a.k.a., Sven the Savage Swede. There were no lights along the rail line at that point, and it was a straight stretch of track where the engineer could "open her up," as much as possible given the limitations of the old steam locomotive and the length of the route.

I hiked to the spot, and as if to confirm my thoughts, the chugging train, shrouded in the 19th century engine's smoke and steam, came pounding past at maybe thirty-five miles an hour, shaking the ground. I found myself being saluted by a long blast on the whistle and a wave from the cab of the locomotive. I saw that he was none other than L. J. Gunderson, the retired Pennsylvania Railroad engineer whom I had interviewed during my very first week at the fair.

The longer I was at the fairgrounds, the more the place seemed like a small village. Everywhere I went, I encountered someone I had interviewed or been served a meal by or had coffee with. Familiar faces abounded, and several times in recent weeks, I got hailed by a wave and the call of "Hi there, *Tribune* man!" I will not go so far as to say these lakefront acres were becoming a second home, but the place was growing on me—up to a point.

That brief feeling of warmth quickly dissipated, however, and I forced myself to refocus on the issue at hand.

CHAPTER THIRTY-NINE

Tomorrow will be the big day, Papa, and I have at last picked the place. Even with all the police roaming the grounds, it is a spot where I will not be disturbed in my work. I am glad it is almost over because I can sense them closing in. I have tried to be careful, but somehow, I feel they have an idea about what is going to happen. But can they stop me before I complete my work? I do not think so. Whatever becomes to me, you will be forever remembered . . .

CHAPTER FORTY

I walked the entire mile-long stretch of Deadwood Central track, then retraced my steps along the route in the opposite direction. I can't say what I was looking for now that I had located the area where I thought any mischief might take place, but I felt that just maybe, I might find some evidence along the way of the rails having been tampered with. I saw nothing amiss, however, and I went home to Oak Park, unsure of my plan for the next day. As it turned out, much of August 4th was to be taken up by unexpected events.

Before I left home the next morning, I reached into the kitchen drawer when Catherine left the room and pulled out our one and only flashlight, slipping it into my suit coat pocket. As I rode into the city on the Lake Street Elevated, I noticed giant black clouds piling up in the sky far to the south. These were darker than any rain clouds I had ever seen. I walked into the press room at the fair a few minutes before 9 to hear my phone ringing. As usual, it was Hal Murray on the city desk.

"Snap, we've got a big one, a huge fire in that Standard Oil refinery down in Whiting. Whatever you've got working right now at the fair, postpone it, cancel it, whatever. We're throwing a whole team into this. I'm looking to you to find human interest angles, the kind of stuff you do best."

"Okay, I gotcha. What's the plan?"

"Doherty's getting ready to drive down there, and you're right on his way. Hold on."

He bellowed across the local room to Jim Doherty, a long-time general assignment reporter. "Hey, Malek's going to ride down with you. Here, I'll put him on so that you two can work out the arrangements. Then I want you out the door and headed south before I blink twice, got it?"

"Okay, Snap," Doherty said into the receiver, "you've had yourself a long enough vacation at the train fair. It's time now for a real story. Where do I pick you up?"

I told him the main entrance, at 23rd Street, and he said he'd be there in ten minutes, fifteen tops. I called Catherine's number at the Oak Park Library to let her know what was going on. She wasn't there at the moment, so I gave the message to a co-worker and went to the front entrance where, thirteen minutes later, Doherty's rusty prewar gray Studebaker lurched to a stop, its brakes complaining loudly.

"Let's burn some rubber," he yelled as I hopped in and we screeched off, heading south on Lake Shore Drive and then city streets, destination: Whiting, Indiana, which lies just across the state line from Chicago's East Side, as it is known to its residents.

The black smoke towering ahead of us obliterated the sky. "Christ, it looks like the end of the world," Doherty said in awe. "I got no idea how close to this we're going to be able to get."

"Jim, I've got a feeling we're going to be *told* just how close we can get," I said.

"Yeah, and maybe even that's closer than we want to be. This nightmare apparently started right around dawn, from what I've been told. Murray's phone call roused me out of bed early. I wasn't supposed to start today until noon."

"I assume we've already got somebody there, right?"

"Thomis, and I think Gowran, too. And one or two photogs as well. Snap, it looks like this is going to be something that one day you can tell your grandchildren about."

CHAPTER FORTY-ONE

As we approached Whiting on Indianapolis Boulevard, the skies grew ever darker until day turned to almost total night, although it was not yet noon. We felt the heat from the fires, turning an already hot day into a hellish one.

"Looks like this will be about as near as we're going to get," Doherty announced as we came to an intersection in a residential neighborhood where a police barricade had been put up. We parked on the street in front of an aged clapboard bungalow and got out, walking in the direction of the smoke and the now-visible flames, a few blocks away.

"Sorry, but nobody's allowed any closer than this," a uniformed Whiting cop on foot told us.

"Reporters, *Chicago Tribune*," Doherty said as we both whipped out our press cards. The young patrolman looked uncertain at first, then nodded soberly and waved us through.

"All right, but be plenty careful, though, boys," he said. "There are still a lot of explosions poppin' off all over the place."

"We should split up now," Doherty told me. "I'm going to meet Thomis at the Salvation Army tent—it's supposed to be at the corner of 119th and Indianapolis Boulevard. You'll be able to get coffee and doughnuts there. I guess you're going to be doing the feature stuff, right?"

"That's the word I got from Murray, and when he barks, I listen."

"Okay, let's see . . . it's 11:05 now," he said, looking at his wristwatch. "How about we meet back here at the car at 3:30?"

"Fine by me," I told him, marching off down a street of bungalows in this resolutely working-class town, notebook in hand. I had looked at a street map of Whiting in Doherty's car as we drove down, so I had a pretty good sense of the small burg's layout.

Sirens were keening off all over the place, and the heat blistered the paint on the houses. A black Pontiac sedan rumbled down the street with four loudspeakers mounted on the roof blaring. "Attention, attention please, everyone keep away from all manhole covers . . . gasoline has entered into the sewer system . . . there's a danger of explosions in the sewers . . . attention . . . attention . . ."

The closer I got to the big Standard refinery, the more I was reminded of the bombed-out streets of Berlin just after the surrender in the spring and summer of 1945, when I briefly served as a foreign correspondent for the *Trib*. I passed a frame bungalow with its screened front porch blown off and lying in splintered ruins in the street. A few doors down, another house had been lifted completely off of its concrete foundation and set back down at a crazy angle, with part of the basement now exposed and most of the windows shattered. God knows what shape the interior was in.

In the next block, an automobile, a '30s-vintage brown De Soto, lay upside-down like a dead animal on the wooden rubble of what until a few hours ago had been a garage.

I came upon a lanky man in a dirty white tee-shirt and Levi's standing in the street gaping at another house that had lost most of its porch and chunks of its shingled roofing. He looked at me blankly and shook his head. "Lord above," he said repeatedly.

"Your place?" I asked.

"Yeah, such as it is."

I flashed my press card. "I'm a *Chicago Tribune* reporter. Is everybody okay?"

"Come down from the big city, eh? Yeah, we're okay, only by the grace of God," he said in a quaver. "We were still in bed this morning when the big blast hit. My first thought was that it was an atomic bomb, like the ones that we dropped on Japan to finish them off back in '45. I was serving on Okinawa at the time those babies hit. When I came home from the war, I thought I was through with explosions forever."

"So, your family. . . ?"

"My wife and little one—she's just four—are okay, again by the Lord's grace. They're with my sister across the state line over in Homewood right now." He jerked his thumb in a westerly direction.

"The National Guard came around and forced us to leave, said there's a chance that the blasts aren't done yet, that they could go on for days, what with all the gasoline that's around. I snuck back to take a look at the place. Other than the porch, I think we'll be okay," he said. If there aren't more explosions, I thought, taking down his name and address.

Farther down, I met another man standing on the sidewalk. He turned out to be a local cab driver, whose own bungalow had been somehow spared.

"*Tribune* man, huh? Yeah, you might say I dodged a bullet, but my next-door neighbor Marty wasn't so lucky—a big chunk of steel pipe flying through the air ripped open one whole side of his house," the cabbie said, gesturing toward a yellow frame cottage whose dining room was open to the air, its table and several chairs shattered by the pipe, which was imbedded in the far wall. "Fortunately, nobody got hit by the pipe," he added.

"Where were you when it all started?" I asked, scribbling notes.

"Just getting up to begin my shift behind the wheel. At first I thought it must have been an earthquake, and so did my wife. I can tell you that the whole house rattled. Right then and there, we both thought we were done for."

"Is your wife all right?"

"Yeah. She's in a Red Cross shelter, pretty shaken but otherwise okay. The soldiers let me come back to see if the cab's drivable. It's got a flat tire and one cracked window, but at least the engine turns over. Not that I'm going to do any driving today, or anytime soon." His laugh had no mirth behind it.

I passed three uniformed, armed National Guardsmen who probably were on the lookout for looters. They gave me questioning looks until I showed my press card, finally putting it under the brim of my hat where it should have been in the first place.

"*Chicago Trib*, huh? I would be real careful if I were you, sir," one of the soldiers said respectfully, taking off his helmet and wiping his grimy brow with an equally grimy handkerchief. "We were just talking to a manager from the oil company, who told us they're all real worried right now that a giant tank of naphtha, three million gallons worth, could blow at any time. The flames keep getting closer to it," he said to us.

"Thanks for the warning," I replied, and no more than fifteen seconds later, an explosion shook the ground, sending a ball of flames rocketing skyward and staggering all four of us with a blast of heat that felt like a giant oven had suddenly been thrown open.

"It's that naphtha tank!" one of the Guardsmen yelled, pointing toward the fireball that streaked across the sky like some spaceship in a Buck Rogers comic strip. "Oh, Lord, I hope that those oil workers left there when we did." Squaring their shoulders, he and his helmeted comrades turned and jogged in the direction of the latest horror.

I spent the next several hours walking the debris-littered streets of Whiting interviewing others who had stories to tell: the woman who was out at sun-up hanging out laundry on a backyard clothesline when the first blast hit, its impact knocking her and all the clothes to the ground . . . the grocer on Indianapolis Boulevard who had gone into his store early to restock his shelves and was there when an explosion blew in both of his display windows . . . the Standard Oil maintenance man who loudly cursed his company's safety measures as he picked up chunks of wood and slices of asbestos roofing that had blown into his scruffy front yard from neighboring houses . . . and the eighty-six year-old pensioner sitting on his front porch who refused to leave his house and told me he "always knew something like this was going to happen with all that damnable gasoline around."

I wanted to ask the old fellow why in heaven's name he had chosen to stay in Whiting, what with all of that damnable gasoline he mentioned, but I figured that given the current miserable situation here, the last thing he needed was some wise-guy Chicago reporter asking such a question.

* * *

At 3:30, I was waiting next to Doherty's soot-covered car when he came up, face blackened by the heat and smoke. "You look like somebody who's ready to do a vaudeville act in blackface," he japed.

"If you could see yourself, you wouldn't laugh," I fired back.

"Oh . . . Geez, yeah," he said as he slid behind the wheel and looked at himself in the rear-view mirror. "Well, they can't say that we didn't see combat. You phoned anything in yet?"

"Nope, never came anywhere near a pay phone that worked. I found one on a street corner, blown over and with a dead instrument inside."

"Well, I managed to call in about ten graphs using a phone hookup at the Salvation Army. You want to stop someplace on the way back and phone the desk?"

I said I did, and we pulled up to the curb at a Rexall drug store along South Chicago Avenue back in the city, our smudged faces drawing stares from the customers sitting on stools at the soda fountain. I slid into a phone booth at the rear of the store, dropped in my nickel, dialed the paper, and talked first to Murray, then dictated a piece to the rewrite desk, which took almost a half-hour.

"I suppose that you're ready to call it a day?" Doherty asked when we were back on the road heading northward.

"No, you had better drop me off at the fair. I've got some unfinished business."

"Well, I'll be damned, this man is a genuine hero!" he said, taking both hands off the wheel briefly to clap. "After surviving the very furnaces of hell, he plunges right back into his beat. Are you angling for a bonus, Snap?"

"That will be the day," I laughed. "Truth to tell, I'm not exactly in love with this fair posting, but maybe if I keep the higher-ups happy, they'll let me go back to playing police reporter again, along with all the big boys like yourself."

"Well, not that my word means anything in the halls of power, but that's just where you belong, Snap, not writing fluff at some exposition. Although I've got to say, the assignment there has ended up being a lot more interesting that you probably figured. If I didn't know better, I'd suspect that you bumped all these people off yourself, just to remind the boys on the news desk that you haven't lost your touch as a crime reporter. Kill 'em, then write about 'em."

"I'm not quite *that* desperate to get my old job back," I answered with a laugh.

"Well, whatever happens, good luck," Doherty said, as he dropped me at the front gate of the fair and rumbled off.

CHAPTER FORTY-TWO

I got more stares as I showed my pass and entered the grounds, heading straight for the nearest men's room. With face scrubbed reasonably clean, I shuffled into the empty press room and dropped into my chair. I stretched my limbs, feeling that whatever energy I had left was about to make an exit and that I was powerless to stop its exodus.

I probably hadn't dozed off for more than a minute or two when my phone rang. Expecting it to be Murray on the city desk, I picked up the receiver and growled "Yes, I'm back, I'm back. What do you need now?"

"Oh, Steve, I'm so glad I got you!" Catherine said breathlessly. "I've been—"

"Ouch, sorry for the rude greeting, my darling. I thought for sure that it was the *Tribune* bugging me again."

"That's perfectly okay, I'm just glad to hear your voice. I've been calling you all afternoon, hoping you were all right. As I know you can imagine, the explosion and fire in Whiting is all over the news on the radio."

"I'm not surprised. It was like nothing I've ever seen—or ever hope to see again."

"You are all right, aren't you?"

"Yeah, a little on the sooty side, you might say, and my face feels like I fell asleep on my back on a tropical beach, but otherwise, all my moving parts seem to be in good working order."

"Good. There's . . . another reason that I'm calling, though."

"Oh?"

"I've been thinking over all the things you've said to me about the people and the goings-on at the fair, and about one name in particular. Anyway, I had a lull at the library early this afternoon, and something just jumped out at me while I was daydreaming. I don't know whether I ever told you this, but for no particular reason, I took a couple of years of German at the good old Oak Park and River Forest High school."

"No, you never mentioned it, but what's the point here?"

"Well, it may really be nothing, but I went back into the stacks at the library to see if my memory was correct."

"Go on. You've got my attention."

"It was correct—my memory, I mean," Catherine said. She then proceeded to lay it out for me. At first, the whole thing seemed preposterous and unlikely, but on the other hand . . .

"That's . . . interesting," I said, digesting what she had told me.

"Steve, you'll take it to the police, right?" Her voice had an edge.

"I'll tell them, of course, but they may just brush it off. Hell, Fahey already thinks I've lost some of my marbles, the way I've been tossing off theories about the killings."

"Well, this may just be a weird coincidence, but I thought that I had better tell you."

"I'm glad you did, and I am going to pass it along to Fergus."

"Will you be coming home soon, Steve?"

"Because of the fire, I've got some catching up to do here. I'll call when I'm leaving."

"Be careful," she said with a quiet intensity, as if sensing that there was more to my "catching up" than I was letting on.

After hanging up, I chewed some more on her "German-English" discovery, and I really did briefly consider telling Fahey about it before discarding the finding as a bizarre coincidence—maybe. I then turned my thoughts to the evening ahead.

Twilight was settling over the fairgrounds as I left the press room and grabbed a cup of coffee and a roast beef sandwich on rye at the counter of Leo's Grubstake Diner in Gold Gulch, which was the southern terminus of the Deadwood Central Railroad. I even got a kosher dill, the quality of which would have pleased Pickles Podgorny.

The faux-Western town, with its hitching posts and raised wooden sidewalks and a main street of false-front frontier-style buildings that included the Silver Dollar Saloon, a nickelodeon silent movie house, shooting gallery, and "Dutch Annie's" waffle shop, was crowded with fairgoers enjoying the balmy evening.

As I left the diner in near darkness, a train filled to capacity with passengers was just arriving at the Gold Gulch station, meaning it would be making the return trip north within the next half hour. That was the run that concerned me on this tenth anniversary of the deaths of three pre-teen boys on their bicycles.

It was completely dark by the time I walked north on a path that paralleled the railroad track. About two blocks north of Gold Gulch, the track diverged from the path, which I left, moving over to the rails.

I turned on my flashlight and played it back and forth across the rails and crossties, wondering whether Fahey had indeed sent more men to the neighborhood of the railroad line because of what I had told him. So far, I hadn't seen anyone who looked remotely like a detective, which probably meant he had dismissed my theory—or Walt Disney's, really—as a crackpot idea.

I went on for a one city block, then another, and another. The tracks were clear. I began to think that Fahey was right, that I was on a fool's errand, the victim, not for the first time, of my own overactive imagination, further fueled in this particular case by the fertile mind of one Walt Disney.

I now had reached the darkest stretch of the Deadwood Central. The nearest streetlights, more than a block away at the North Western Railway's Paul Bunyan exhibit, did not penetrate the trees in this seeming wilderness-within-a-city. The footing was uneven on the graveled roadbed of the line, and I stumbled and nearly fell twice but recovered my balance.

The second time I righted myself, my flashlight beam caught something on the track ahead. It was numerous iron bars several feet long, reinforcing bars like those used in building construction. Lashed together by metal cable into bundles of two and three each, they were wedged at angles between and on the rails. I'm no expert on this sort of thing, but they looked like they could easily force a train off its tracks.

I knelt and pulled one of the bundles of bars off the track, heaving it over against the base of the stockade fence separating the fair from Lake Shore Drive just to the west. Then as I tossed a second bundle off the tracks, my name was called.

CHAPTER FORTY-THREE

"That's enough, Mr. Malek—stop right there!" The familiar voice came from a cluster of bushes some twenty feet east of the tracks. I spun around and saw a shadowy figure emerge from the foliage with a gun in his hand.

"Well, if it isn't Mr. Rob Taylor—or should I say Schneider?" I said in a voice turned suddenly hoarse.

"It is Taylor," he snapped, moving slowly towards me, a revolver trained on my midsection. The earnest, engaging youth I had come to know these last few weeks had transmogrified into a hard-edged avenger who now seemed far older than his years.

"Taylor translates to Schneider in German, correct, Rob?" I said, licking my lips.

"It does when you spell it T-A-I-L-O-R," he answered curtly. "I'm surprised that you have a working knowledge of German."

"I don't, but I had some help. So, here we are," I said, working to keep my voice calm and swallowing to generate saliva in a desert-dry mouth. "As you can see, someone very carelessly put things on the track that could do some real damage, Rob."

"How did you find out?" he sputtered, moving to within a yard of me.

"I didn't until just a little while ago," I told him, gauging the distance between us and maintaining eye contact. "All along, I figured it was either the guy whose name apparently is Whitnauer or possibly your boss, Fred Metzger."

Rob cut loose with a joyless laugh, keeping the revolver trained on me with a steady hand. "That's really funny," he said, "funnier than you could possibly know."

"I was not trying to be a comedian."

"First, there's Whitnauer. I know you figured out that he was the one who called himself Samuel White."

"Perhaps by overhearing some of my telephone conversations through the paper-thin walls of the administration building?"

"Yes, sir, Mr. Snap Malek, right you are. Mr. Whitnauer, by the way, is no longer with us."

"Meaning?"

"Meaning that he had an accident a few days back. He was very helpful to me early on, as I guess you are aware."

"By putting a live round into a rifle, the round that killed a young and innocent actor."

"Yeah, for which he was well rewarded," Rob said bitterly. "But it wasn't enough. He wanted more money, the greedy bastard."

"And if he didn't get it, I suppose he was going to tell his story to the police."

"So he claimed when he called me at the fair about a week or so back. At first I didn't believe him, because I figured that if he did talk, it would go hard on him, too. But he was an ignorant man, illiterate, actually. And I couldn't be sure . . ."

"Mr. Malek, get out of my way now. I'm going to put that material back on the tracks," Rob said, gesturing with the gun.

"Indulge this old newspaperman's curiosity, Rob. Tell me what happened to Whitnauer."

"Let's just say that I paid him a visit in his . . . hotel room, if that's what you could call that pigsty. I told him I was bringing more money, but when I got there, I started by giving him a pint of cheap booze."

"Which he was glad to see?"

"Damned right. He was a pathetic tosspot. He drank right from the bottle, drained it in fifteen, twenty minutes."

"And then. . . ?"

"Do you even have to bother asking?" Rob said with a smirk. "The rest was easy."

"You strangled him?"

"Nope. He wiggled the revolver that was aimed in my direction as if to indicate how Whitnauer died.

"That makes a lot of noise."

He smirked again. "Mr. Snap Malek, in that part of Uptown, nobody even pays attention to a gunshot."

"So you used that," I said, nodding toward the revolver.

"Oh, no. Poor Sam, he killed himself. Last I saw, he was lying on his bed with the gun in his hand. He left a printed suicide note, confessing to his sins."

"Printed, of course, so the handwriting couldn't be checked."

Rob shrugged. "That's part of it. Also, Whitnauer could barely write his name, so I figured a guy like that, well, the best he could do would be to print. And I made plenty of spelling mistakes in the note."

"So you killed a destitute illiterate and four others if you count the actor, all to avenge . . . who, your father? Do I have that right?"

"Don't talk about my father!" he yelled, waving the pistol. "You don't know anything about it."

"What about Metzger? Where does he fit in?" I asked.

"You mean Uncle Fred, former last name Schneider? Oh, he knew what was going on the whole time. You might say he was my accomplice in all of this, although he hasn't got much stomach for what I was doing. In fact, he's cringing back in his office right now, waiting for me to come back and tell him how everything turned out."

"I must say that you two put on some pretty damned good acting jobs for me after a couple of the deaths."

"Well, for me it was acting," Rob said, "although in Uncle Fred's case, he really did get shook up each time something happened. He didn't even know that I'd hired Whitnauer to put a live round in that rifle. But after that, he had to go along with everything else. Besides, he hated what the railroads did to my father—his brother—every bit as much as I did."

"And of course you got the job at the fair through your uncle."

"You might say that in a sense, he got the job at the fair through *me*. You remember the name Chester Rawlings?"

"The man who did public relations at the fair last year?"

"Yes. He had an unfortunate accident in a subway station."

"An accident that you had a hand in, no doubt."

"No comment."

"So the job at the fair was open, and Fred, who already had a public relations form, applied for the position. What if he hadn't gotten it?"

"Interesting that you should ask, but then, you're a skilled reporter. I like to think I'm a very good planner. After the fair ended last season, I went to visit Mr. Rawlings in his office, looking for a job. While there, I managed—it wasn't hard—to filch a piece of his stationery and an envelope. The very day of his fatal accident, the Railroad Fair received a letter from him on his letterhead saying that he had a serious heart condition, and that should anything happen to him, he highly recommended Fred Metzger for the position."

"Incredible."

"Thank you, I thought so," Rob said smugly. "But lest you think I'm totally cold-blooded, let me remind you what life was like after my father's train hit those boys."

"It had to be rough," I said.

"You can't possibly know—nobody can. Now, Mr. Snap Malek, I'm going over to the tracks. Don't try to stop me. I'll take care of you later." Rob skirted around me, keeping the gun trained on my stomach. Backing up, he went over to the fence to get the iron reinforcing bars that I'd thrown there.

He bent to pick up one of the bundles with his left hand, and his gun barrel was briefly pointed down as he bent over. In that instant, I heaved my flashlight at him, and my years as an outfielder with a neighborhood baseball team paid off. I scored a direct hit on his right temple. He groaned and the gun discharged as he put his other hand to his forehead.

His second groan was louder, more of a scream, really, and I realized that he had shot himself in the leg. He keeled over and I was on him in an instant, picking up the revolver and pulling the last of the iron off of the rails as he lay beside the tracks writhing and moaning.

"My father was over forty when I was born," Rob said through gritted teeth, "but he still should be alive today. He'd be only sixty-six, if only things hadn't been . . .

"You couldn't begin to imagine what it was like," he went on, the words coming in gasps. "After the . . . accident, everybody . . . everybody hated my father. Called him names . . .

painted swastikas on my parents' sidewalk, or on their doors. Broke the windows with rocks. The neighbors asked us to move, said we were bringing violence to the block.

"We moved again . . . but we couldn't hide, and the harassing went on. No railroad would hire him . . . he tried, tried again. They all said he had mental . . ."

Rob grimaced in pain and gripped his leg. I retrieved my flashlight, which surprisingly still worked, and played it on his pants, where blood had begun to soak through.

Rob's next groan was accompanied by blinding pain—my pain! My face was raked by something sharp and hard. The revolver, I later figured out. Rob had picked it up off the ground, where I had carelessly set it down, and he slashed it across my forehead, opening a gash that sent blood spurting down into my eyes.

I must have yelled, although everything from that moment on for the next several minutes became a blur in more ways than one. Still groaning, Rob dropped the gun and crawled to where the bundles of metal lay, trying to drag them back onto the tracks.

I got up, felt the world spinning, then dropped to my knees, wiping blood out of my eyes. Now I was crawling, too, and we engaged in what might laughingly be called a wrestling match if it hadn't been such a pathetic performance on both our parts.

I'm pretty sure I grabbed him by the shoulders and forced him to let loose of the metal bars. He then drove a fleshy fist into my face. There wasn't much force behind the punch, but it was enough to knock me back and start another eruption of blood, this time from my nose. As I struggled to right myself, the train's whistle sounded from the south.

Rob heard it, too. The ground began to vibrate slightly, and he made one last effort to pick up the bars. Failing, he began to cry, his sobs sounding like hiccups. The ineffective headlight beam of the old locomotive materialized down the tracks and became larger.

He swung his fist one last time, a blow to my arm that I barely felt, although he followed it with a shove that pushed me away from the track. Half crawling, he scrambled past me and, too late, I realized what was happening.

As the locomotive pounded toward us, it loomed larger to me than it had seemed before, perhaps because it was night and I was on the ground just an arm's length from the tracks. Just before the coal-burning, smoke-and-steam spewing beast thundered past, Rob threw himself onto the rails. The only scream I heard was my own.

CHAPTER FORTY-FOUR

The high-pitched screeching still haunts me the most, that nerve-jangling sound of steel-on-steel, or whatever surfaces they use for the brakes on vintage trains. I rolled over on my side and found myself staring at the wheels on one of the passenger cars of the Deadwood Central train. Above me, I heard the chattering voices of the passengers.

"Oh dear, what's happened?" "Why did we stop so quickly?" "I almost fell off my seat." "Look, what's that poor man doing lying down there, bleeding and everything?"

"That poor man" happened to be me. I stood on rubbery legs, anxious to get as far away as possible from being the center of attraction for the riders on this fated run.

I walked up to the panting locomotive. Its engineer and fireman had climbed down out of the cab and were talking to a man in a rumpled business suit, who turned out to be none other than Homicide Detective Jack Prentiss.

". . . and I applied the brakes as quickly as I could," one of them was saying breathlessly. "But . . . but, I couldn't stop, I . . . Oh, how is he?"

"Looks to be dead," Prentiss said. "But it is not your fault, not at all."

"I killed a man," he wailed. I recognized him as L. J. Gunderson, the retired Pennsylvania Railroad engineer who I had interviewed weeks ago.

"The detective is right, Mr. Gunderson," I said. "It is not your fault. You shouldn't worry about what happened. I was there, I saw it all. The man your train hit threw himself onto the tracks. He's a mass murderer. He killed—"

"Hold on right there!" Prentiss bellowed, red-faced, the veins standing out in his neck. "This is strictly a police investigation, and you got no business being here, and shooting off your yap, Mister Newspaper Hotshot. By the way, you look like holy hell."

"You would, too, Detective, if you had been rolling around on the ground wrestling with an armed madman and trying to stop him from derailing this train," I yelled back. "His name is Rob Taylor, although it used to be Schneider. He is an intern in public relations here, and he's behind the killings at the fair, every damned one of them. His uncle, Fred Metzger, who's the public relations honcho at the fair, is an accomplice and chances are you can find him in his office in the Administration Building right now."

Prentiss shot me a glance that made it clear I was not welcome anywhere within his sight. "If you want to talk to me about this, I'll be in the fair's press room after I've cleaned up," I snarled to him over my shoulder as I limped off.

In the men's room, using paper towels, I did the best job I could of cleaning the caked blood off my face. Then I went to the fair's dispensary, where a grandmotherly-type nurse in a starched white uniform swabbed the cut on my forehead and applied a bandage to it.

"You look like you have had yourself quite a fall," she said with genuine concern.

"Yes I did, but it could have been a whole lot worse." I thanked her and went to the press room, just in time to see a blubbering Fred Metzger in handcuffs being escorted out of his office by two uniformed cops and a detective. He looked at me and shook his head between sobs.

At my desk, I immediately dialed Catherine.

"I was wondering when I'd hear from you," she said. "Are you coming home soon, Steve?"

"I'm going to have to stay a little longer, my love. There's been some trouble, and the police want to talk to me."

There was a pause of several seconds, while she exhaled. "Are you all right?"

"Absolutely, never better—although I did run into a little snag here and there. Everything seems to have worked itself out, though. I'll fill you in when I get home."

I could tell she wasn't satisfied with my explanation, but I insisted that everything was fine and told her I had to go to a meeting before I could leave the fair. Just as I was hanging up, my "meeting" filled the doorway of the press room. It was, of all people, a grim-faced Chief of Detectives Fergus Sean Fahey.

"I've seen you looking better," he observed, lumbering in and slumping into a swivel chair at the rarely used *Daily News* desk.

"Well, if this isn't a switch now!" I said with bonhomie. "*You* visiting *my* office. Well, I'm nothing if not a good host, Fergus. I just happen to have a pack of Luckies with me," I told him, tossing them over along with a book of matches from the Rock Island Lines' "Fiesta" dining car.

He lit up and considered me. "I'm here because I didn't want to send Prentiss to talk to you, given the feelings you have for each other. There's been enough violence at this damned fair. Now that I'm here, I don't know whether to congratulate you or chew you out," he murmured.

"Well, I'll accept congratulations, if that will help you decide," I told him, lighting up myself. "I take it from what Prentiss said that Taylor is dead."

"Train hit him, as I guess you know. Didn't run over him but knocked him clear. The impact did the job, though. Why didn't you let us know what you were doing?"

"Frankly, because I didn't think anyone would believe me. But also, I sort of expected to see some of your men patrolling the Deadwood Central tracks after what I said about today being the anniversary of those kids' deaths."

"Well, something happened to change things," Fahey said in a low voice. "Whitnauer is dead. His body got found today. I tried to call you here several times and got no answer."

"I was otherwise occupied, at a refinery down in Whiting."

"Oh, yeah, right. Some of our uniforms are down there now, helping out the local force. Anyway, it turns out that Whitnauer had been dead for days. People living in that flophouse in Uptown smelled, well . . . you know what they smelled, and it was not a rat. Somebody finally broke into the locked room and then called us. It looked like he shot himself."

"Which was how it was supposed to look," I said. "Taylor told me about how it all happened just before he made his final move. By the way, Fergus, how did our intrepid Mr. Prentiss happen to show up along the track so soon after Taylor got hit?"

"Somebody heard a shot and told one of the uniformed men

on the grounds. He went to Jack, who happened to be on duty tonight, and . . ." He turned a palm over.

"I can tell you a lot about that shot, Fergus." I proceeded to describe those last frantic minutes leading up to Rob Taylor's death.

Fahey looked for an ashtray and, failing to find one, flicked the ashes from his Lucky onto the plank floor, grinding them under his heel. "So, what made you suspect this Taylor in the first place?"

"As you know, I had what at first seemed like an out-of-left-field idea that the fair killings were the work of somebody seeking revenge against railroads—all railroads. So I went through the *Trib's* clips on train mishaps, and that 1939 case of the three kids on bikes getting killed by a train jumped out at me.

"I mentioned this to my wife, whom you have of course met, and gave her all the details, including the name of the train's engineer, Schneider. Earlier today, Catherine called me and said she had looked up 'Schneider' in a German-English dictionary and found that it translates to 'tailor.' in our very own mother tongue. Schneider was also the original last name of Fred Metzger, Rob's uncle and the PR head at the fair who your guys hauled out of here in cuffs a few minutes ago."

"I know," Fahey said, leaning back and running a hand through his hair. "So these guys were both related to the engineer?"

"His son and his brother. As Rob and I were struggling like two kids on a grade school playground a few minutes before he died, he told me how his father had been persecuted by the parents of the dead kids, among other people. He was a German immigrant, and still spoke with an accent.

"After the accident, he couldn't find work on any railroad—they all apparently figured he was a mental case. On top of that, he got called all sorts of names, including 'Nazi,' and his houses were vandalized. I say *houses* because the family moved a couple of times to get away from the harassing. They never did escape it, though, and the old man finally hanged himself in his basement."

"I gather Taylor was behind the shooting at the pageant, too?" the chief posed.

"Yeah. He either had a hand in hiring Whitnauer, or 'Sam White' if you prefer, at the fair or got to him once he was working there. Then, and maybe your men will find out how, he got hold of a live round and had Whitnauer load it into one of the rifles."

"He couldn't possibly have known that a single shell would kill someone, though."

"No, he got 'lucky' there, if you can use such a word to describe a tragedy. The fellow who fired the fatal shot, as I think you know from his questioning, had been something of a hunter as a kid, shooting ducks with his father out along the Mississippi River. He knew his way around weapons."

Fahey nodded. "And I gather from what you started to say a minute ago, Rob Taylor told you about the flophouse shooting?"

"He did, figuring that I wasn't going to be around to tell anyone else about it. He admitted the killing and said he also printed the 'suicide' note."

"So you were right. He didn't want the handwriting traced back to him, or compared against Whitnauer's."

"I was only partly right, Fergus. Sure, Taylor didn't want the handwriting checked against his own. But as to comparing the note to Whitnauer's writing, it wasn't going to happen. The poor bastard couldn't read or write."

"Jesus. He killed an illiterate?"

"Yeah. And for what it's worth, I'll give you a theory—unprovable, of course. I think Taylor may have originally planned only the shooting at the pageant nothing more. When that resulted in a death and garnered all manner of publicity, he got excited and emboldened and realized he could wreak really big-time revenge against the railroads. So, he started his killing spree."

"Maybe," Fahey said. "Like you said, we'll probably never know. As long as you're dealing out theories, why do you figure Taylor killed the illiterate? Was the guy going to squeal?"

"So Taylor claimed to me. He said Whitnauer wanted more money or he'd go to the police. That may or may not be true, though. I'm afraid I may be indirectly to blame for what happened. As you can see, the walls in this place are just plywood, and it's not hard to hear between rooms, especially if you're trying to. Metzger's office is right next door, and it was easy enough for him and his nephew to overhear my phone calls. You'll recall I talked to you about Whitnauer." I did not bother to add that I'd also discussed him on the phone with Pickles Podgorny.

"At that stage, I had no idea whatever that Taylor was our man, with his uncle as an accomplice," I went on. "So I inadvertently ended up playing right into their hands."

Fahey lit another Lucky and watched the smoke rise toward the ceiling. "We'll go though the office, of course, and both their homes. Do you know anything about whether either one was married and had a family?"

"I have no idea. He never mentioned anybody. The fair's executive office probably has the particulars on Metzger, and maybe Taylor as well."

"Another question, and here I'm just asking for your speculation: Do you think Taylor planned to kill himself right from the start?"

"No. I believe he threw himself in front of the train only after I had prevented him from sabotaging it. He was beaten and he knew it, so he may have seen killing himself as his only option."

The chief scowled. "What a nightmare this has turned into."

"True, but at least the killings are over now."

"That may be, but there's likely to be all manner of investigations, both within the department and by the those civic do-gooder groups that like nothing more than to let us know they are not happy with our performances."

"A lot of tut-tutting, right?"

"All that and a lot more, Snap, including periodic cries for change in the upper echelons of the department You've been around long enough to know how that works. It's pretty predictable. Well, I've got to touch base with the commissioner, among others," he said without enthusiasm, rising slowly and walking out into the night.

CHAPTER FORTY-FIVE

My phone had squawked twice while Fahey and I were talking, but I ignored it. I was pretty sure that at least one of the calls had been from the *Tribune*, so I dialed the city desk. To my surprise, Hal Murray was still manning his post.

"I didn't expect to hear your voice this late," I told him. "Not that I'm in any way disappointed, you understand."

"Are you by chance still at the fair?" he barked. "I called you a couple of times."

"You might say that I've been tied up for awhile. The killer—make that alleged killer—of three people out here is now dead himself, as you probably know by now. Plus he's an accomplice in a fourth death here."

"You're damned right, we know. But we don't know a whole lot else, except that the police are saying that a suspect in that pageant shooting was found dead in his hotel room in Uptown today. What've you got for us?"

"Quite a bit. I can tell you more about that Uptown death, and I also was an eyewitness to a suicide, but I don't want a big deal made out of my role. I had more than enough of that during the Truman business last fall. I'm well aware that we are expected to report the news, not make it."

"That's true, although you seem to be the exception to that rule," Murray remarked dryly. "You are to news as a pot of honey is to a hungry bear. Look, just feed Williamson everything you've got, and the higher-ups here can do the worrying about whether there is too much of you in it."

"Aye, aye, sir. Put Mr. W. on, and I'll regurgitate what I've been experiencing here on this fine Chicago summer evening."

I gave Williamson all the gory details, and being a superb rewrite man, he as usual asked a question after almost every sentence I dictated.

"Look Eddie, please play down my part in this," I beseeched him.

"Okay, but we have got to keep in that eyewitness description of Taylor throwing himself onto the tracks. You know that the bosses are going to want that. It sells and it shows the world that the *Tribune* is always right where news happens. Let the other papers try to match *that*."

I groaned, but knew he was correct. He did promise, however, to keep my role at a minimum. However, his wasn't the ultimate decision by any means. That was made Pat Maloney and the other top editors sitting at the big, four-sided desk in the center of the newsroom.

The next morning, the *Tribune's* banner headline read FAIR KILLER ENDS LIFE! The lead story gave a straightforward account of Taylor's killing spree and death, but sure enough, the editors had included a sidebar that was headed TRIB REPORTER SEES SUICIDE. It used practically every quote that Williamson had wormed out of me when I had phoned in.

"Dammit all!" I said as I read the paper at home while drinking coffee after breakfast. Catherine had decreed that I was in no condition to go to work at the fair that day, and I did not argue the point. She had been beside herself the previous night when I got home well after 11 o'clock and she took one look at my face.

Her initial shock gave way to anger, which I'm happy to say quickly gave way to concern. There was the requisite "I thought you said that you wouldn't get involved . . ." admonishment, but she then rapidly switched into Florence Nightingale mode, which I accepted as being a pretty good outcome after what had been one of the wildest days of my life.

"He actually was going to kill you, wasn't he?" Catherine posed as we had more coffee.

"It was on his mind," I said, "but for some reason, I wasn't worried, although I'm not sure that I can tell you why. Rob Taylor seemed so singularly intent on wrecking that train that I became almost an afterthought, a minor irritant."

"Yes, but you were the only one standing in the way of making the wreck happen."

"I suppose that you're right. He darned near pulled it off at that. He would have if he didn't take his mind off of me, if only for an instant. Even at that, I had to make a perfect throw with our trusty flashlight."

"Who would have thought it would come down to a flashlight? In the end, it all gets back to Walt Disney's theory being right on the mark," Catherine said as she looked at me over the rim of her cup. "Now what, Steve?"

"What do you mean?"

"Will you go back to the fair after all this?"

"I really don't know; that's up to the editors. I'll tell you this, however. I think we've pretty much milked the thing dry. There are only so many features you can wring out of an exposition like this. I thought when I got the assignment that it was overkill."

"You didn't say anything to your bosses at the time, though."

"True enough. But it pretty much got presented to me as a *fait accompli,* as you will recall."

"You were plenty depressed then."

"Well, I'm still not exactly doing handsprings now about my future prospects," I told her. "And to top it off, I wake up to find the home-delivered edition full of my exploits. Just what a reporter doesn't want to be: A major player in a story he's covering."

"But don't your editors have to be impressed with you now. Won't all of that publicity actually help what you refer to as your 'future prospects'?" Catherine asked.

"I don't know . . . maybe," I replied, draining the rest of my coffee.

"We will just have to worry about those future prospects later," she said with wifely authority. "Right now, I want to change the bandage on your forehead and put another cold compress on your nose. He could have broken it."

"True, but given its original Slavic configuration, almost anything would be an improvement," I said as we went upstairs, where she would further minister to my wounds, both physical and psychological.

CHAPTER FORTY-SIX

After a one-day recuperation at home, I persuaded Catherine that I had recovered enough to return to the fair. It seemed strange to walk into the press room knowing that Fred Metzger and Rob Taylor would never be back, although as I started to sit down, heard noises coming from next door.

A slender, balding man in a business suit whom I did not recognize was going through the filing cabinets and other papers in the public relations office. He turned as I entered.

"Oh, hello, hope that I am not disturbing you," he said amiably. "My name is Gene Hayes, I'm one of the many assistant managers at the fair."

He held out a hand, and as we shook, I introduced myself. "Oh yes, Steve Malek, everybody here knows you, especially after what happened two days ago. I believe you are the only full-time newspaperman on the grounds, isn't that correct?"

"Yes it is. Is there anything I can do for you?"

"Oh—now that the police have, er, finished going through this office, I've been sent in to see what's in the files and also to try to figure out just how we are going to cover public relations during the last few weeks of the run."

"Afraid I can't suggest a PR boss for you, although I can recommend an assistant."

"Really? Who might that be?"

"Her name is Charlene Miller, and she's a student at Mundelein College up on the North Side. She currently is working as one of the ticket sellers at the main entrance, but clearly she's being wasted there. She was a great deal of help to me a few weeks ago on a project, and I highly commend her. She's lively, eager, and a quick learner."

"Well, that's very thoughtful of you, Mr. Malek. I'll look into it today. Thank you so much."

As it turned out, Charlene spent the rest of the fair's run working as a public relations assistant to a bright young man who was brought in from one of the local P.R. firms. I got the impression seeing them in the office next door that they might end up being more than working colleagues.

I now faced the problem of figuring out where my next feature was coming from. I might just have to begin wandering the grounds in search of interesting people and events. Or maybe I could start leading tours, showing visitors where the various murders had taken place.

My reverie got interrupted by the telephone's jangling. "Snap, have you got a few minutes to talk?" It was Fergus Fahey.

"For you, always. To what do I owe this unexpected pleasure?"

"Your colleague Westcott, and of course by extension the others in the press room here, all know what I'm about to tell you, but I figure that I owe you an update."

"I guess maybe you do at that. Shoot."

"We went through Metzger's office there at the fair, but we found nothing of interest. Ditto his home, but Taylor's place was quite another story."

"Hmm. Where did he live?"

"With his mother, on the Far South Side—the house they moved to not long after Josef Schneider's suicide."

"Find anything interesting?"

"Just wait till you hear. We got a search warrant, and a team rifled the place. The mother went into hysterics as our men rifled through her dead son's effects, and she had to be restrained by a matron who fortunately had been brought along. She swore in both German and English the whole time our dicks were there. Even taught them some new curse words.

"But enough of that. There were several notebooks filled with Taylor's hand-written ravings—I don't know how else to describe them. A lot of it consisted of diatribes against the railroads and how they had destroyed his father."

"The young guy turned out to be a real case," I observed.

"Yeah. He also had a fat scrapbook filled with clippings from every newspaper in town about the accident, the inquest, and a follow-up investigation by the railroad that cleared his father.

"Speaking of his father, one of these notebooks, the spiral-bound kind that students use, had nothing in it except notes and letters to the old man."

"That's interesting. He had saved them all these years, huh?"

"No, that's just it! He had been 'writing' to old Josef Schneider right up to the other day. Every letter neatly done in longhand."

"Weird, all right," I said.

"These letters, some just a few sentences, others a page or two, described how he was going to kill somebody at the fair. Others were written after the deeds had been done, so to speak.

He kept repeating how he was doing all of this as a way of avenging his father."

"My God, that's macabre. You know that the papers are going to love this."

"There's more. I don't know if you remember, but the man who headed up public relations at the fair last year died after he fell off a subway station platform in the Loop and got hit by a train that was just pulling in."

"Fergus, I think that I know what you're going to tell me."

"Maybe you do at that. "One of Taylor's hand-written epistles, if you want to call them that, was about Mr. Chester Rawlings and how he happened to fall onto the subway tracks."

"Let me rake a wild stab. He was pushed by one Rob Taylor, who had hinted as much to me on that last awful night."

"Here, I owe you this. Let me read from his notebook: *Chester was such a very nice man, a very gentle man, Papa, and I truly hated what I had to do. Truly I did. I had followed him for several days, getting used to his habits. Finally, he was right where I wanted him to be. The platform at the Monroe Street stop was crowded, and he was standing very close to the edge. Wonderfully close to the edge. I reached in with one arm and gave a nice, strong shove just as the train entered the station, then I merged back into the crowd as they all began screaming. I don't think he felt a thing. But I had no choice, Papa. I had to fulfill our destiny.*

"How is that for macabre, Mr. Deadline Man?"

"It ranks right up there. As I said before, the papers are going to love this. They'll all run wild with it in tomorrow's editions and in the days to come. Is the heat off of you and your bosses now?"

"Sort of," Fahey said sourly, "although the Crime Commission and the other civic groups are claiming that we should have got onto Taylor a lot sooner. They don't say how we should have known about him, but then, they're great at playing the old 'Monday morning quarterback' game. Sooner or later the quote 'poor police work' is bound to turn up in at least one of the papers."

Fahey was right, as so often the case in his predictions about the press. The exact quote, from the head of the Crime Commission, did indeed pop up in a *Sun-Times* story the very next morning. I was also right, not surprisingly, in my own prediction that the papers would have a picnic with the discovery of Rob Taylor's maniacal writings.

FAIR KILLER'S RAVINGS BARED! was the *Trib* banner, while the *Sun-Times* went with LETTERS REVEAL MIND OF YOUNG MADMAN! Even the normally sedate *Daily News* could not contain itself, opting for MURDERER WROTE DAILY TO DEAD FATHER, while Hearst's *Herald-American*, as was to be expected, topped everybody with DEPRAVED KILLER SPELLED IT ALL OUT FOR US!

CHAPTER FORTY-SEVEN

After devouring all the stories in the four papers at my desk in the press room, I reached a long-distance operator on my telephone and gave her a California number that I had kept on a neatly folded sheet of paper in my wallet.

After the second ring, a cultured female voice informed me that I had reached "Mr. Walt Disney's office."

When I identified myself, she acted like I was an old friend whose call had been anticipated. "Oh yes, I will put you right through, sir," she said crisply.

"Ah, Mr. Malek, it is so good to hear from you," Walt Disney said in a hearty tone. "Do you bring me some news from your grand Railroad Fair?"

I told him I did and proceeded to relate the saga of Rob Taylor, from his father's tragic life all the way through to the grim finale on the fairgrounds, ending my narrative with: "So you absolutely were right, Mr. Disney. You had it all figured out correctly, and because of you, a lot of lives surely were saved."

"Well, this is a very sad story," the filmmaker said, "but I am glad that you were there to prevent what would have been a far worse tragedy. Also, I want to relay all of this to Ward Kimball, who as I told you in Chicago often accuses me of indulging in flights of fancy. Although I must say in these tragic circumstances, I take no pleasure in having been correct. "

"Nonetheless, this particular flight of fancy of yours turned out to be an arrow that made a direct hit on the bulls-eye," I said. "The fair certainly owes you a debt of thanks, although they may never know it."

He laughed. "I would rather they didn't know it. The people at the fair owe me nothing, Mr. Malek. They gave me so much pleasure when I was there that if anything, I am in their debt, and they are most surely in your debt. Have you recovered from your injuries?"

"Yes, they were superficial at most. I appreciate your concern."

"You might be interested to know that since I've been back here, I have begun thinking in earnest about my amusement park," Disney said. "I can't begin to tell you how many ideas I've gotten from the Railroad Fair that I plan to incorporate in the park."

"So you can call the trip a success in more ways than one?"

"Indeed I can, Mr. Malek. And if you ever find yourself out here in beautiful Southern California, I insist that you look me up. I would like to give you a tour of our studio, and perhaps someday, of our new amusement park as well. I'll need to come up with a name for it, though."

"I believe that it should have your name somewhere in the title," I said, as much to humor him as anything else. It still sounded like a half-baked idea to me.

CHAPTER FORTY-EIGHT

Not surprisingly, the last few weeks of the Chicago Railroad Fair were more than a little anticlimactic for me. Oh, I still cranked out stories all right, some of them actually suggested by the new young P.R. man and the enthusiastic Charlene Miller, both of whom had stepped up and filled at least some of the public relations void left by Fred Metzger and Rob Taylor.

A few examples: An interview with a grizzled seventy-nine-year-old gold miner, who had panned for the stuff during the Klondike Gold Rush in the Yukon in 1897 and spun his yarns, some of them possibly true, at the "Gold Gulch" frontier town; a talk with a mid-season newcomer to the outdoor ice show, a thirteen-year-old skating sensation from suburban Glen Ellyn, who outperformed many of her older and more seasoned colleagues; and a profile of Janie Brady Jones, the octogenarian widow of locomotive engineer Casey Jones, who visited the fair almost a half-century after her legendary husband's death in a storied rail collision on the Illinois Central down in Mississippi.

I looked forward to the closing of the fair in early October for a pair of reasons. First, of course, the assignment I got maneuvered into was ending; second, and far more important, was a date that I had down in Missouri shortly after the fair's end.

"Glorious" best described that sunny October Saturday in the well-heeled St. Louis suburb of Clayton. In the back yard of a handsome Georgian-style house, a white canopy crowned by brightly colored streamers stood out against the backdrop of a rolling green lawn.

The blue-robed minister stepped forward and opened his book to begin the litany of the marriage ceremony for Amanda Gail Rogers and Peter Reed Malek. As we all stood on the grass under the canopy for the short service, I glanced at Catherine to my right and saw a bit of moisture in her eyes, then looked to my left at Norma and noticed the same. My former and present wives, united in their emotions.

I danced with four women on that fine afternoon: Catherine, Norma, Amanda, and Amanda's mother—more dancing than I had done in one day in probably twenty years. Amazingly, not a single toe got stepped on, which probably was more a tribute to the ladies' dancing prowess than to mine.

After a honeymoon in San Francisco, the newlyweds would begin their lives together in a spacious four-room apartment in the Lakeview neighborhood, not far from Wrigley Field, and they would commute on the Howard Elevated Line to their Downtown jobs: Amanda's in the 19th Century European Art Department at the Art Institute and Peter's at the renowned architectural firm of Skidmore, Owings & Merrill.

CHAPTER FORTY-NINE

I now was a man without an assignment—and very possibly without employment of any sort whatever. The Monday morning following the wedding, I ventured to Tribune Tower at the request of Managing Editor J. Loy (Pat) Maloney, reasonably certain that I would receive my walking papers from him.

Maloney was on the phone when I got to the paper's imposing two-story local room. He indicated with hand gestures that he would be tied up for awhile. While waiting, I shot the breeze with Hal Murray and also with Eddie Williamson, the ace rewrite men to whom I had dictated so many stories from the Railroad Fair in recent days.

I then plopped down just outside Maloney's glassed-in office for what seemed like an hour but was probably closer to twenty minutes. He finally cradled his receiver and beckoned me in with a wave of an arm.

"Mr. Malek," he said as I parked myself in a guest chair, "sorry for the delay, but when Colonel McCormick calls, that takes precedence, as you know. Well, you had yourself quite a summer out there at the fair, haven't you? Not exactly what any of us had bargained for, was it?"

"No sir, it certainly wasn't."

"You did a fine job, though, a fine job. Mr. Murray sang your praises to me on more than one occasion. And you are of course aware that he doesn't hand out kudos willy-nilly. So the assignment turned out to be quite a success, especially given that you were not exactly eager to take it on, were you?"

"To be honest, no, I wasn't, as you could probably tell when the subject first came up."

"I would expect nothing less than honesty from you, Mr. Malek. And you would expect nothing less than honesty from me, is that correct?"

"That's right," I said, sucking in air. Here comes the hammer, I thought. Time to learn a new trade, if that was possible at my age.

Maloney leaned back, lacing his hands behind his head in what for him was a characteristic pose, especially when he was about to make a pronouncement. "Mr. Murray and I were talking about you earlier this morning. It is his firm belief, and I highly esteem his judgment, that you can be of the most value to the Tribune at Police Headquarters. Do I gather that you concur with that belief?"

I must have let out a cubic yard of air out before answering. "You gather right, sir."

"Good, good. I'm happy to hear that. The we are of one mind."

"What about Westcott?"

Maloney smiled. "I thought that you would probably ask, as you have always been known for your interest in the welfare of your colleagues. You'll be interested to learn that Mr. Westcott is going back to general assignment reporting."

"Is he okay with that?"

"He is indeed. I know you were on vacation last week. Something about a wedding, as I recall. I trust the happy occasion went well."

"Yes it did," I replied in a raspy voice. "I now have a wonderful daughter-in-law."

"Good, I'm so glad to hear that. Would you be able to report at Police Headquarters on . . . oh, let's say, next Monday?"

"I will report there whenever you tell me to, Mr. Maloney."

"Then next Monday it is," he said with a disarming smile, standing and pumping my hand. "Oh, and Mr. Malek?"

"Yes, sir?"

"When you are back on the job at Headquarters, please give my warmest regards to Chief Fahey. Our paths crossed many times years ago, when he was a much-decorated sergeant and I was a young police reporter."

"I will sir," I said.

One week later, I walked into the press room at Headquarters and received . . . a standing ovation!

"We heard a rumor that you were coming back, Snap," Packy Farmer said, "but we weren't going to believe it until you walked through that doorway. Westcott wouldn't tell us a damned word about it, but a funny thing happened here last Wednesday, didn't it, Dirk?"

"Yeah," O'Farrell said, "except it was Thursday. I was going out to lunch, and down in the lobby I ran into Fahey's cute little secretary, Elsie. She smiled at me and said, 'Well, I guess you'll all be happy with the change in the press room next week, won't you?'

"When I looked puzzled, she said something like, 'Oops, I guess maybe I talked out of turn, didn't I? Please ignore what I said.'"

"Just what do you make of that, Snap?" O'Farrell asked.

"I don't know, but it sounds like I was just about the last one to know what's been going on here lately."

"Well, now that you're back," Anson Masters said after clearing his throat, "maybe the rest of us will have a better idea of what's going on down in the Detective Bureau. To say the least, we were not terribly well served by your replacement, Mr. Westcott."

"So I have been led to believe."

"Well, enough of the raillery," Masters said. "It's time for all of us to get to our beats."

I walked down the one flight to Fergus Fahey's office, where I was greeted by Elsie Dugo Cascio's dazzling smile. "Welcome back—for good, I trust!" she said, squeezing me. "At the risk of being seen as forward, I must tell you that you have been missed!"

"Thank you. I missed you as well. I do have a question, though."

"I'll see if I have an answer."

"By any chance, did your esteemed boss at any time in the last several days make a call to, or receive one from, Mr. J. Loy (Pat) Maloney, the esteemed managing editor of the *Chicago Tribune*?"

Elsie pouted. "You know very well that I'm not at liberty to answer that question. You will have to ask him yourself."

"I will do just that," I said, pulling a new pack of Lucky Strikes out of my suit jacket pocket as I swung open the door to the office of Chief of Detectives Fergus Sean Fahey.

AUTHOR'S NOTES

The preceding is a work of fiction and all of its principal characters, other than those listed below, are my own creations. Also, all of the instances in which historical characters interact with fictional ones are strictly products of my imagination.

Walter Elias ("Walt") Disney is one of the giants of U.S. cinematic history. His company's 1930s and 1940s productions, among them "Snow White and the Seven Dwarfs," "Dumbo," "Pinocchio," and "Fantasia," set the gold standard for animated films, and through Disney cartoon shorts and comic books, the irascible Donald Duck and the amiable Mickey Mouse became indisputable American cultural icons.

In addition to films, the Disney machine expanded into television, first with a highly rated weekly show and then with the purchase of the ABC television network. Today, the Walt Disney Company is the largest media and entertainment conglomerate in the world, with annual revenue in the billions of dollars. The company's theme parks, beginning with the opening of Disneyland in Anaheim, Cal., in 1955, are also in Florida, France, Japan, and China.

Walt Disney attended the Chicago Railroad Fair with Ward Kimball in 1948, although I used literary license and moved the visit to 1949, the fair's second season. In his 2006 book "Walt Disney: The Triumph of the American Imagination," Neal Gabler wrote that Disney's visit to the Railroad Fair helped inspire him to create Disneyland.

Disney, a heavy smoker, died of lung cancer in December 1966, a week after his sixty-fifth birthday.

Ward Kimball, who attended the Chicago Railroad Fair with Walt Disney, is widely recognized as one of the legendary figures in film animation. An Academy-Award winner, the man whom Disney termed a "genius" created several of the animated characters on Disney films, among them Jiminy Cricket in "Pinocchio," Lucifer the Cat in "Cinderella," and Tweedledum and Tweedledee in "Alice in Wonderland." Kimball, who worked for the Disney Studios from 1934 until the '70s, died in 2002 at the age of eighty-eight.

John C. Prendergast began his 43-year career with the Chicago Police Department in the first decade of the Twentieth Century. He served as police commissioner from 1945 until his retirement in 1950. He died in 1958 at the age of seventy-four.

J. Loy (Pat) Maloney started his *Chicago Tribune* career in 1917. Over the years he rose steadily through the ranks at the paper and became its managing editor in 1939 on the death of Bob Lee. He directed the *Tribune's* news coverage throughout

World War II and into the Post-War era, retiring in 1950 for health-related reasons. He died in 1976 at the age of eighty-five.

Harold (Hal) Murray was a longtime newsman with the *Tribune*, joining the paper in 1934 after working at the City News Bureau of Chicago. For the *Trib*, his reporting beats included City Hall and the Criminal Courts. He then became an editor, and was day city editor on his retirement in 1971. He died in 1995 at the age of eighty-eight.

Martin H. Kennelly was mayor of Chicago for two terms, from 1947 to 1955. He came into office as a "reformer" following the corrupt regime of his predecessor, Edward J. Kelly. Kennelly proved too independent to suit the Democratic bosses, however, and he was defeated in a primary by the candidate favored by the party machine—Richard J. Daley. That marked the beginning of a Daley dynasty that continues to this day in the form of Richard M. Daley, who, like his father, has served more than 20 years in the position.

The Whiting, Ind. Refinery Fire. Serious students of Chicago history will note that as with Walt Disney's visit to the Railroad Fair, I moved this occurrence to 1949 from its actual date. The multi-million-dollar fire and subsequent explosions took place in August of 1955 and laid waste to much of the 1,600-acre Standard Oil of Indiana refinery just south and east of Chicago along the shores of Lake Michigan. Fortunately, there was little loss of life, although hundreds were injured and more than 1,000 residents of Whiting were temporarily evacuated from their homes, many of which were destroyed or damaged.

I took descriptions of the event from newspaper reports, including the terrifying naphtha explosion and ensuing fireball that rocketed into the sky, as well as the auto that landed upside down on the ruins of a garage.

Train Mishaps. Three of the train wrecks referred to were historical: The 1918 Hegenbeck-Wallace Circus train disaster near Hammond, Ind.; The 1921 collision between two passenger trains in Porter, Ind.; and the 1946 tragedy in Naperville, Ill., in which one Burlington Route passenger train rear-ended another. There was heavy loss of life in all three. The fourth mishap mentioned, in which three boys were killed by a freight train, was purely fictional.

The Chicago Railroad Fair of 1948 and 1949, celebrating the centennial of railroading in the Windy City, was sponsored by thirty-eight railroads and the Pullman Company and occupied 50 acres of land along Lake Michigan south of Downtown Chicago. It was the last such exposition of its scope, and marked the final time such a vast array of vintage operating railroad equipment was brought together in a single place. The fair was considered a success by its organizers and by the railroads in general. According to the *Chicago Tribune*, "The Railroad Fair has been successful far beyond the expectations of the men who started it." It was reported that in its two seasons, the fair drew more than 5.5 million visitors.

ACKNOWLEDGMENTS

As with my four previous Snap Malek novels, I relied heavily on the microfilm files of the daily newspapers, particularly the *Chicago Tribune*, for information on news, sports, politics, personalities, and major events of the era including of course the Chicago Railroad Fair. As a long-time journalist, I confess to an inbred bias toward newspapers, a medium that continues to struggle. But to me it remains the best prism through which to view contemporary society and its vagaries.

Also of great help in jogging the memory of one who attended the fair several times as a ten-and eleven-year-old from the Chicago suburbs were two collectors' items: The slick 1948 and 1949 fair programs (cost: 35 cents), both of which provided valuable details on the displays, exhibits, and geography of the fair, as well as illustrations and other information on specific railroads that were represented.

Another helpful source of information was Neal Gabler's 2006 biography, "Walt Disney: The Triumph of the American Imagination" (New York: Alfred A. Knopf, 2006).

This volume was particularly valuable in its descriptions of the trip that Disney and Ward Kimball took to the Chicago Railroad Fair in 1948. Also, as mentioned above, Gabler stressed the fair's importance in helping to form the moviemaker's vision of Disneyland and of the company's subsequent theme parks.

In addition, a tip of the hat to long-time friend, poker-playing colleague, and ace competitive marksman Ray Rausch, who was helpful with details relating to the vintage firearms that played a role in the narrative.

ABOUT THE AUTHOR

Robert Goldsborough is an American author best known for continuing Rex Stout's famous Nero Wolfe series. Born in Chicago, he attended Northwestern University and upon graduation went to work for the Associated Press, beginning a lifelong career in journalism that would include long periods at the *Chicago Tribune* and *Advertising Age*.

While at the *Tribune*, Goldsborough began writing mysteries in the voice of Rex Stout, the creator of iconic sleuths Nero Wolfe and Archie Goodwin. Goldsborough's first novel starring Wolfe, *Murder in E Minor* (1986), was met with acclaim from both critics and devoted fans, winning a Nero Award from the Wolfe Pack.

THE SNAP MALEK MYSTERIES

FROM MYSTERIOUSPRESS.COM
AND OPEN ROAD MEDIA

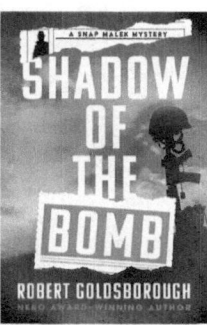

MYSTERIOUSPRESS.COM

THE MYSTERIOUS BOOKSHOP, founded in 1979, is located in Manhattan's Tribeca neighborhood. It is the oldest and largest mystery-specialty bookstore in America.

The shop stocks the finest selection of new mystery hardcovers, paperbacks, and periodicals. It also features a superb collection of signed modern first editions, rare and collectable works, and Sherlock Holmes titles. The bookshop issues a free monthly newsletter highlighting its book clubs, new releases, events, and recently acquired books.

58 Warren Street
info@mysteriousbookshop.com
(212) 587-1011
Monday through Saturday
11:00 a.m. to 7:00 p.m.

FIND OUT MORE AT:

www.mysteriousbookshop.com

FOLLOW US:

@TheMysterious and Facebook.com/MysteriousBookshop

OPEN ROAD
INTEGRATED MEDIA

Find a full list of our authors and
titles at www.openroadmedia.com

FOLLOW US
@OpenRoadMedia